BB

"Where am I?"

"In the hospital ... Garett Memorial," Frank told her.

"No, I mean what city? What state?"

"You don't know?" he asked.

She shook her head, the motion making her realize it throbbed with a dull intensity.

"You're in Garett Beach, North Carolina."

He had a wonderful voice, she thought. Deep and soothing, like a fire on a wintry night, it promised a comforting warmth. "How ... how did I get here?"

"I brought you here. You collapsed on the beach outside my house." Compassion stirred in Frank as he saw the confusion that muddied her green gaze.

It was obvious she didn't remember anything of how she came to be here. It was also a safe bet that she didn't remember the single moment the night before when she'd connected with him in a way he couldn't forget....

Dear Reader,

Welcome to another month of top-notch reading from Silhouette Intimate Moments. Our American Hero title this month is called *Keeper,* and you can bet this book will be one of *your* keepers. Written by one of your favorite authors, Patricia Gardner Evans, it's a book that will involve you from the first page and refuse to let you go until you've finished every word.

Our Romantic Traditions miniseries is still going strong. This month's offering, Carla Cassidy's *Try To Remember,* is an amnesia story—but you won't forget it once you're done! The rest of the month features gems by Maura Seger, Laura Parker (back at Silhouette after a too-long absence), Rebecca Daniels and new author Laurie Walker. I think you'll enjoy them all.

And in months to come, you can expect more equally wonderful books by more equally wonderful authors—including Dallas Schulze and Rachel Lee. Here at Silhouette Intimate Moments, the loving just gets better and better every month.

Happy reading!

Leslie Wainger
Senior Editor and Editorial Coordinator

Please address questions and book requests to:
Reader Service
U.S.: P.O. Box 1325, Buffalo, NY 14269
Canadian: P.O. Box 1050, Niagara Falls, Ont. L2E 7G7

TRY TO REMEMBER

Carla Cassidy

Silhouette®

INTIMATE MOMENTS®

Published by Silhouette Books

America's Publisher of Contemporary Romance

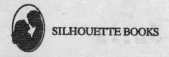 SILHOUETTE BOOKS

ISBN 0-373-07560-X

TRY TO REMEMBER

CARLA CASSIDY

is the author of ten young-adult novels, as well as her many contemporary romances. She's been a cheerleader for the Kansas City Chiefs football team and has traveled the East Coast as a singer and dancer in a band, but the greatest pleasure she's had is in creating romance and happiness for readers.

To Alfie and Sally—partners in plot.

Prologue

She walked along the beach, struggling to keep her balance as the undertow sucked the sand from beneath her feet. Moonlight shimmered on the water, dancing on her skin with its pale, ghostly light. A ghost, yes, that was what she was...a restless spirit with a tormented soul who could find no peace.

She stumbled, fell to one knee, not caring as she ripped her nightgown. She'd given up caring a long time ago. The last six months of her life were a blur.

She sank backward onto the sand, allowing the waves to lick at her toes, caress her calves. The sand still retained the day's heat, warming her backside, but it wasn't enough to penetrate the chill that gripped her soul.

She frowned suddenly, trying to remember if she'd taken two sleeping tablets or three. Not that it mattered. Lately it seemed to take more and more of the little pills to achieve sleep, and even then she couldn't find peace.

Escape... that was what she yearned for, to escape from the nightmares that plagued her nights, to get away from the memories that haunted her days. If she could just stop the relentless screaming in her head, hush the death cries that tortured her.

She reached up and let her fingertips touch the taut scar tissue on her neck and shoulder. She stared up at the full moon, then closed her eyes against the overwhelming anguish that filled her heart.

Chapter 1

Dr. Frank Longford sighed with pleasure as he parked his sports car in the driveway of his beach-front cottage. Friday night and he wasn't due back at the hospital again until Monday morning. The week-end stretched before him, promising plenty of cold beer, hours of lazing in the sun and enjoying the latest novel by his favorite mystery author. He couldn't remember the last time he'd managed to have a whole weekend to himself.

"Just what the doctor ordered," he said with a grin, unlocking his front door and stepping inside. He was greeted by his two housemates, each jumping up on him with furry front paws. "Hi, Mutt...Jeff..." He gave each dog an affectionate pat, then walked over and opened several windows, allowing the cooler, salt-tanged air to flow in.

Then, grabbing a cold beer from the fridge, he popped the tab and stepped out onto the back porch. Mutt and Jeff hit the beach like animals possessed, chasing each other with the abandon of children. He watched them for a moment, then took a deep drink of the cold beer.

Breathing another sigh of satisfaction, he pulled off his suit jacket, yanked impatiently at his tie and settled into a chaise longue. His gaze immediately searched the deserted stretch of beach, even though he knew it was too early for her to make an appearance.

It was strange really, how much the young woman who walked the beach each night had managed to capture his imagination. Her routine had been the same since the first time she'd appeared nearly a week before.

She only came out when darkness had fallen and the moon provided the only illumination. She never walked close enough to his house for him to discern much about her. He guessed that she was fairly young simply by the grace of her movements. Even though she wore a billowy, shapeless gown, he could tell she was quite slender.

He wondered what forces drove her to the relentless pacing. It was the same sort of agitated stalk that marked the people in waiting rooms anxious to hear the outcome of a surgery procedure on a loved one.

"Mutt, Jeff... back," he ordered, watching in satisfaction as the two mixed-breed dogs came running toward him, their tongues hanging out from their exertions. He got them back in the house, knowing how much they loved to torment the evening beach joggers, then settled into his chair.

He leaned his head back, relishing the tactile pleasure of the cool evening breeze lightly caressing him, the chill of the beer can in his hand. The wind chimes hanging at the side of the house tinkled softly and provided a pleasing background music to the evening.

He must have dozed off, for when he opened his eyes again, night had fallen and his beer can was warm. He rubbed his eyes tiredly and looked down the beach, unsurprised to see his mystery lady in the distance.

He frowned, noticing that on this night there was no evidence of the graceful movements he'd admired before. Instead, she seemed to be in the middle of a slapstick comedy routine, unsteady on her feet. At one point she fell to one knee, then pulled herself up like a jerky marionette in the hands of an inexperienced puppeteer.

He watched with interest as she lay down and stretched out on her back, like a vestal virgin offering herself as a sacrifice to the gods of the ocean. What in the hell was she doing?

Minutes passed. The wind chimes spoke to the ocean, and the waves answered back, thundering a rhythmic reply. Frank's gaze didn't waver from the strange scene.

He had no idea how much time had passed before he decided something wasn't right. His common sense told him not to get involved, that it was none of his business. The woman obviously hadn't expected an audience, thus her choice of waiting until after dark to venture out. But his doctor instincts told him something was horribly wrong. The woman was in need of help.

Decision made, Frank hit the beach at a dead run, struck by a sudden urgency that burned his insides. He didn't stop until he was about ten feet from where she lay, then he slowed, reason swallowing instincts.

What if she simply enjoyed sleeping on the beach? Maybe it was all some sort of religious ritual. He dismissed each of these thoughts as he advanced on her.

"Miss . . . ?" he called tentatively, standing almost directly above her. The only answer was the ocean's roar, and the faint music of his wind chimes in the distance.

As Frank gazed down at her, he immediately realized several things. As a man, he noticed the classic beauty of her features . . . well-defined dark eyebrows arched attractively over her closed eyes. Her cheekbones were prominent in her slender face, her nose straight, her mouth full and inviting.

As a doctor, his mind quickly assessed different facts. She was much too thin, and her complexion in the moonlight shone unhealthy, waxy and without color.

He leaned down and shook her shoulders, noticing that the tide crept up beneath her as if trying to lay claim to her unmoving body.

Adrenaline shot through him as he picked up her wrist and searched for a pulse. Her skin was cold, clammy beneath his touch. Where the hell was her pulse? There! There it was, thready and dangerously weak. She was in trouble.

Assessing his options, he quickly scooped her up in his arms, the action causing her head to loll to one side, exposing a section of scar tissue that covered the lower portion of one side of her neck and disappeared beneath the shoulder of her gown. He felt a moment's curiosity, then shoved it out of his mind. The scar was old, too old to be the cause for her present unconscious condition.

He ran for the house, pausing there only long enough to grab his car keys. He placed her gently in the back seat, then climbed in behind the steering wheel and started the engine.

From the beach house to the hospital was exactly a twenty-minute drive. On this night, he made it in twelve minutes flat. He used his car phone to call ahead so he would be met at the emergency entrance.

As he pulled up, he was relieved to see the reassuring sight of an awaiting stretcher, several nurses and Dr. Russ Waylon, his friend and colleague, who was the physician on duty.

"Any changes since you called it in?" Russ asked as they headed inside.

Frank shook his head, not taking his eyes off the woman who lay so deathly still on the stretcher.

"I'll let you know as soon as I know something," Russ said, then, with a reassuring smile, he disappeared, along with the stretcher, into the emergency room.

Frank eyed the lime green swinging door indecisively. He could go in. He was a doctor on staff. But he knew his mystery lady was in good hands with Russ.

And she is a mystery, Frank thought as he walked into the waiting room and sat down on one of the bright orange, molded plastic chairs.

It took only minutes for impatience to gnaw at him. He shifted on the chair. It felt strange to be in this position, sitting here instead of on the other side of the swinging door, actively dealing with life and death.

The room was small, and as he sat there it seemed to grow even smaller, closing in on all sides. He now understood why people in waiting rooms paced. There was little else to do to work off the impotent frustration and sense of helplessness.

He rose from the seat and began to walk the short distance of the room, becoming aware that his shoes and socks were filled with sand. With a grimace of distaste, he sat back down, pulled off the loafers and peeled off the gritty socks.

"Hey, Dr. Longford, I heard you were in here."

Frank looked up to see Cindy Manors leaning against the doorframe, her gamin face sporting a huge grin. "Hi, Cindy." Frank stood up, feeling awkward in his bare feet. "You're looking well," he observed, noting the healthy brightness of the young girl's blue eyes.

"I feel good, thanks to you." She smiled at him with all the hero worship a sixteen-year-old could muster.

"What are you doing here at this time of night, anyway?" Frank asked, picking up his shoes and carrying them over to the trash basket, where he dumped out the sand.

"Mom's getting off work in just a few minutes so I'm here to pick her up." Cindy frowned. "What are you doing?" she asked, watching as he began to shake out his socks.

"Oh, I took a little run on the beach earlier," Frank said, deciding not to tell the rest of the story. Garett Beach was a small place and there was no sense starting up a bunch of gossip about his "mystery lady."

She rolled her eyes. "Doctor, you're not supposed to run on the beach in your good shoes," she admonished.

"I'll keep that in mind," Frank returned, sitting back down and pulling his socks on. He looked at Cindy fondly. "And you make sure you look both ways before you walk across a street."

Cindy blushed. "Don't worry, I learned my lesson the hard way." She looked at her wristwatch. "Well, I'd better go. Mom hates to be kept waiting." With a wiggle of three fingers, Cindy left.

Frank watched her go, a sense of satisfaction coursing through him as he remembered the shape she'd been in four months earlier. An impulsive dart across a street had resulted in Cindy's being hit by a car. Frank had been the emergency doctor on duty when she was brought in.

Suffering a broken leg and various bruises and contusions, the girl had been more frightened than seriously injured.

It had taken him a short while to treat her physical injuries, much longer to reassure her, comfort her. The end result was a healthy Cindy, both mentally and physically.

He shoved thoughts of the young girl out of his head, focusing instead on the woman who lay on the other side of the swinging door. Who was she? Where had she come from? What was wrong with her? Hopefully Russ would have some answers for him soon.

As he put his shoes back on, he thought of her face, so delicate, so beautiful in the shimmering moonlight. If only he hadn't waited so long to run to her. If only he'd gone out to talk to her when he'd first noticed her unnatural walk.

He jumped out of his chair as Russ entered the room, a look of bewilderment on his face. "I really don't have much to tell you, Frank," he said, sighing with the weariness of a man who'd already worked ten too many hours.

He motioned Frank to sit down, then he sank into the seat next to him. "Her vitals are stable. We sent blood to the lab for a drug screen. She's slightly malnourished, but I can't find one good reason for her to be in this near-comatose state." Russ grimaced. "Of course, if we had a better neurological department, more modern equipment, we could run more complete tests."

"So, what's the next move? Wait for the lab results?"

Russ nodded. "I figure if they come back negative, then we'll have to call Wilmington and get their neurosurgeon to come down and do some extensive testing."

Frank nodded, comfortable with Russ's decision.

"So what's the deal?" Russ asked. "You didn't say much when you called it in. Who is she?"

"Your guess is as good as mine. She was walking the beach near my place. I saw her stumble and fall. She got back up, walked a few steps and then stretched out on the beach. When she didn't get up, I ran to her and brought her in."

"Did she hit her head when she fell?"

Frank shook his head. "Not that I could tell."

Russ frowned. "Ten to one it's drugs or alcohol."

A denial jumped to Frank's lips, but he swallowed it instead of voicing it. What did he know about her? Her condition could very well be drug-related. "Can I see her?"

"Don't see why not," Russ said with a shrug. "We're keeping her in intensive care until she regains consciousness."

Frank nodded and stood up, running a hand through his hair in distraction. He started toward the doorway, but paused as Russ called to him. "You know this isn't like the old Chinese proverb...the one that says something about, if you rescue someone, you're then responsible for them for the rest of their life."

"I know. I don't feel responsible," Frank protested. "Besides, I have enough trouble being responsible for those two mangy mutts of mine," he finished with a grin.

But minutes later, standing over her bed, Frank couldn't help but feel a certain amount of responsibility toward his mystery lady.

She looked so frail, so beautiful with her dark hair splayed across the white of the pillow. She was like Sleeping Beauty after her finger had been pricked with the poisoned needle. Frank fought a sudden impulse to lean over and gently touch his lips to hers. Would that pull her from her world of darkness? He scoffed inwardly at his own foolishness. She wasn't Sleeping Beauty and he definitely was no prince.

As he stood there, looking down at her, studying her features, he found himself wondering what color her eyes were. Brown probably, given the darkness of her hair. Or blue . . . that would be particularly striking.

"What's up, Doc?" Etta Maxwell, one of Garett Memorial's most efficient nurses walked in, smiling fondly at Frank. "I heard you brought in a fallen sparrow." She looked down at the deathly still woman on the bed. "I take that back. This one is no plain sparrow, she's a real beauty."

Etta fussed with the blankets like a mother hen clucking over a sick chick. "We're going to fix you right up," she said, her voice a soothing melody that calmed the most colicky baby, charmed the crabbiest of patients. "You're in good hands with Doc Frank here," she continued, smoothing the long dark hair with gentle, wrinkled hands. "He's a doctor who cares...cares too much sometimes, if you ask me," she added beneath her breath.

"Etta," Frank said in friendly warning. He and the older nurse had had this argument many times in the past.

"Well, it's true," she retorted, the grayness of her eyes matching the color of her short, curly hair. "You let patients suck the blood right out of you." She gently plumped the pillow beneath the woman's head. "But don't you worry none, pretty lady. That's what makes him such a good doctor. He'll heal your broken wings and soon you'll be flying off to where you belong." Etta checked the IV site, then straightened up and eyed Frank critically. "You should go on home and get some rest. You look like hell."

"Whatever happened to the concept of nurses respecting doctors?" Frank grumbled good-naturedly.

Etta cackled a laugh. "That concept went out when we nurses realized doctors weren't saints...they're just men, and like all men they can be real pains in the butt at times." With another burst of her infectious laughter, she left the room.

Frank swallowed his smile and shook his head ruefully. Etta Maxwell was the most well balanced, centered woman he'd ever known. Widowed for over ten years, irreverent to a fault, she was a favorite in the hospital, known for her big heart and common sense approach.

He looked again at the woman on the bed, surprised to find himself looking into the greenest pair of eyes he'd ever seen. Green . . . he hadn't even considered that possibility.

Then, realizing she was awake, he moved closer. "Hi, I'm Dr. Longford," he said softly, not wanting to frighten her.

But there *was* fear in her eyes. Not fear of him, but some inner torment so intense her wide eyes shimmered with it.

She reached out a hand to him and Frank took it, feeling the desperation in her grasp. "Help me," she breathed softly, her gaze echoing the plea.

Before Frank could respond, her eyelids closed once again and the hand he held in his went slack, lifeless.

Frank released his breath, unaware until this moment that he'd been holding it. He was shaken, much more so than he'd been in a very long time. Her appeal had been more than one of patient to doctor. It had been that of a tormented soul reaching out for help, and Frank knew, at that moment, that he had to do whatever was in his power to help her.

She awoke suddenly. Without opening her eyes she knew she was in a hospital. The smell surrounded her, an antiseptic mixture of rubbing alcohol and industrial-strength, pine-scented cleaner. Sounds seemed muted, a rolling cart whispered down a long hallway, the murmur of voices from another room, the buzz of someone ringing for a nurse. Yes, definitely a hospital. But why was she here?

Wiggling her fingers and toes experimentally, relief surged through her. At least everything seemed to be working properly. She was in no pain. So why was she here?

Somebody entered her room... a woman with one squeaky, rubber-soled shoe. She could tell it was a woman by the gentle lilac scent that suddenly filled the room, the whisper of nylons rubbing together. A nurse, she decided as she listened to the sounds of the window shades being pulled up.

She cracked an eyelid, for a moment her vision blurry and unfocused. She opened the other eye and squinted, bringing into focus a short, plump, gray-haired nurse who was making notations in a chart. As she watched, the nurse closed the chart and slid it into the holder at the end of the bed.

"Oh, lordy me. You're awake," she exclaimed, clasping a hand to her heart, obviously startled. "I'll just go get Dr. Longford. He'll be so pleased."

She scurried out and the woman on the bed turned her gaze to the window. The sunshine streaming in was brilliant, radiating warmth as it made dancing patterns on the bed. Summertime? She frowned. What had happened to spring? Where had winter gone?

She turned her head, sensing rather than hearing somebody in the room. He stood just inside the door, a doctor judging by his white coat and the stethoscope dangling around his neck.

He was very attractive, with dark hair just beginning to gray at the temples. His eyes were the color of melted caramels, and when he smiled she felt a strange familiarity, as if she'd met him before in some distant dream.

"Hi," he said, moving closer to the side of the bed, bringing with him the pleasant scent of a spicy aftershave. "I'm Dr. Longford . . . Frank Longford."

"Hi," she replied, struggling to sit up, surprised to realize she didn't have the strength. "Where . . . where am I?"

"In the hospital . . . Garett Memorial."

"No, I mean what city? What state?"

"You don't know?" he asked, his forehead wrinkled in concern.

She shook her head, the motion making her realize it throbbed with a dull intensity. She raised a hand and gently massaged her left temple.

"You're in Garett Beach, North Carolina," he answered.

He has a wonderful voice, she thought. Deep and soothing, like a fire on a wintry night, it promised a comforting warmth.

"How . . . how did I get here?" she asked, pressing at her temple once again.

"I brought you here. You collapsed on the beach outside of my house." Compassion stirred in Frank as he saw the confusion that muddied the green of her gaze.

It was obvious she didn't remember anything of how she'd come to be here. It was also a safe bet that she didn't remember that single moment the night before when her eyes had opened and she'd connected with him in a way he couldn't forget.

All night long after he'd returned home, he'd thought about that look in her eyes, the desperate tone of her voice as she'd asked for help. It had haunted him like nothing had before in his life.

He smiled at her. "How about I ask some questions now," he suggested. She nodded and he continued. "How do you feel?" He pulled up a chair by the side of the bed and sat down.

"Like I fell from the sky," she answered with a rueful smile.

The smile, curving up her sensual lips and lighting her green eyes, caused Frank's heart to do something strange in his chest. "Could you be a little more specific?" he asked, pleased by her show of a sense of humor.

"There really is nothing specific except for the fact that I have a terrible headache. Other than that, I just ache and feel so weak."

He nodded. "Your weakness is probably a result of the fact that you're slightly undernourished. The headache and achiness can be attributed to the traces of sedatives the lab found in your blood."

"Sedatives?" Her dark eyebrows drew together in a frown. "You mean like sleeping pills? That's ridiculous, I don't take sleeping pills."

There was so much righteous indignation in her protest, Frank decided not to pursue the topic.

"When can I be released?" she asked.

Frank frowned. "Dr. Waylon is your official doctor and I think he wants to keep you here for a couple of days of observation."

She nodded, almost apathetic in her agreement to the suggestion.

"Finally, the most important question of all. When I brought you in here, we couldn't find any kind of I.D. You were dressed in a nightgown and didn't have a purse, or anything. I don't know your name."

She removed her hand from her temple and stared at him, her eyes like the muddied waters of a deep, mysterious pond. "Neither do I," she replied softly.

Chapter 2

Her name...what was her name? She searched the recesses of her mind, trying to tear away the dark layers that obscured her identity. She closed her eyes, waves of confusion washing over her as she found nothing but blackness where her memories should be.

"I don't know...I can't think..." She heard the edge of hysteria in her own voice, feeding the panic that climbed up her throat and threatened to choke her. She swallowed convulsively against it, refusing to give in to it.

She frowned, staring at the doctor...Dr. Longford...why could she remember his name, but couldn't remember her own? Again the panic crept up the back of her throat.

"Let's try something else," he said, his voice gentle. He moved his chair closer to the edge of her bed and again she caught the pleasant scent of his cologne. Drakkar. Why was it she instantly knew the name of the cologne, but couldn't remember her own damned name? "What can you tell me about yourself?" he asked.

She shook her head, an overwhelming helplessness sweeping through her as she realized she couldn't answer his question. Her mind was a horrifying blank. She knew nothing about herself, where she came from, nothing. Who am I? The words screamed in her head. *Who am I?*

She took a deep breath, trying to control the shivering she felt in her body. What had happened to her? Why was she here? What was her name? The questions echoed in the blankness of her head, terrifying her.

"Can you tell me today's date?"

She felt her frown deepen. She could hear her heartbeat throbbing in her temples, hear a dull roaring in her ears. "No," she whispered.

She felt the tears burning behind her eyes, and she willed herself not to cry. If she gave in to the horror and started to cry, she was afraid she would never be able to stop.

"It's all right," he said softly, squeezing her hand with his larger one. "We'll run some tests, see what we can find. But don't worry, I promise you it will be all right."

And somehow, looking into his warm brown eyes, she felt her anxiety fading. Yes, somehow, *some way*, it would be all right. Dr. Frank Longford would make it all right.

But minutes later when he left her room, she turned her head and stared out the window, the fear once again stealing in to fill her with a kind of controlled panic.

Her name. It was a simple thing...*should* be such a simple thing. But the absence of that single bit of information made everything incredibly complicated, intensely frightening.

Garett Beach, North Carolina. She wouldn't even be able to pinpoint its location on a map. Was it her home? Did she live here? "Garett Beach, North Carolina." She spoke the words aloud thoughtfully, waiting for a ring of familiarity to go off in her head. There was none.

The tears she had held back before now trekked unchecked down her cheeks. She tasted their saltiness on her lips, swiped them away impatiently, her fingertips lingering as she felt the curve of her cheeks, the prominent ridge of cheekbones.

Not only did she not know who she was, but she had no idea what she looked like. She ran her hands down the sheet that covered her. She was thin...too thin. She could count her ribs, feel the slightly protruding hip-bones. For some reason, the thinness didn't feel right. It didn't feel normal.

She drew in a deep breath and fought off another wave of panic. She felt as if she'd been thrust into a stranger's body. Maybe she was a pod person, but the aliens in charge had made an error. They had forgotten to transplant her brain.

She felt a hysterical burst of laughter bubble to her lips, but instead of releasing it, she swallowed it. Terrific, so far she'd managed to remember the name of a men's cologne and an old horror-movie plot. She was making progress. This was a nightmare... a horrible nightmare.

Summoning what little strength she had, she shifted her legs over the side of the bed. She needed a mirror. If she didn't know who she was, she could at least see what she looked like.

She was as wobbly as Bambi on ice, her legs shaky as she made her way across the floor toward the bathroom. What had happened to her? Had she been in an accident? She clung to this thought. Yes, that must be what had happened. She'd hit her head and it had caused some sort of temporary amnesia.

Once in the bathroom, she leaned weakly against the sink. She closed her eyes for a moment before peering into the mirror.

Surely if she saw her reflection, her memory would instantly return. Surely if she saw her own face staring back at her from the mirror, she would instantly recall her name, reclaim her identity. Hope welled up inside her as she raised her head and stared at her reflection.

Long black hair framed a narrow face, emphasizing large green eyes. The nose was small and straight, the lips full and generous. It was a nice face, but it was that of a complete stranger. "Dear God," she whimpered as her initial hope escaped her on a tortured sigh. "Who am I?"

She started to turn away from the mirror, then paused as she caught sight of a scar. It started at the base of her neck and disappeared into the top of the hospital gown. She pulled at the garment, seeing where the mottled, pale scar ended on her shoulder. She jerked the gown back up, her knees so weak she grabbed the edge of the sink for support.

What sort of an accident would have caused such an injury? And why couldn't she remember? Why couldn't she remember anything at all?

"Ah, there you are, dearie." She turned to see the little gray-haired nurse standing in the bathroom doorway. The nurse took the young woman's arm firmly and led her to a wheelchair that awaited by the door of the room. "You should have rung for help if you needed to get up. That's what I'm here for. I'm Etta Maxwell, and you need anything at all while you're here, you just ring that buzzer and I'll come running."

As Etta chatted, she helped the younger woman into the wheelchair. "Now I'm going to run you down to the lab. Dr. Waylon has ordered all kinds of tests for you. He and Doc Longford will fix you up. They're good doctors, both of them."

As Etta pushed her down the corridor of the hospital, she tried to find comfort in the nurse's words. Surely Dr. Longford would find out what was wrong with her. They'd give her a shot or a pill and restore her memory. She had no other choice but to trust in their expertise. She clasped her hands together tightly in her lap, hoping, praying, that Dr. Longford could give her back her identity, her life.

"Nothing. I see absolutely no physiological cause for her amnesia," Frank said, staring at the test results in front of him. Russ had reached the same conclusion only moments before, and Frank looked at him in frustration. It had been almost forty-eight hours since he'd brought her in, hours spent in running tests that would determine any conceivable basis for her amnesia. The neurosurgeon had come in from Wilmington earlier that day and had run more extensive tests, and the results had all come back within the normal range.

"Her CAT scan is normal, her blood workup is okay, no severe vitamin deficiencies, no suspicious bumps on the head." Russ scratched his cheek and shrugged his shoulders. "If I had to guess, the only thing left is some sort of psychological problem."

Frank nodded absently. "At least we now have a name," he said. The hospital had contacted the police, who'd gone to the rental cottages and discovered that the woman had signed the register as Jane Smith. The police had gathered up her belongings and brought them to the hospital. Unfortunately, in those meager belongings there had not been a purse, a wallet or any official form of identification.

"So, what do we do now?" Frank asked Russ.

Again Russ shrugged. "There's nothing more we can do for her here. The next step is to release her."

"Release her? Release her to what? She has a name, but no memory, no real identity. She has no money, no I.D. What's she going to do?"

Russ frowned. "I'll call Social Services and see what they can do for her. Surely they can put her up in a shelter, or something."

"When are you releasing her?" Frank asked.

"I see no point in putting it off. This afternoon. In fact, I was just going in to tell her."

"I'll tell her," Frank said, knowing instinctively it would distress her to leave what had been a safe and known environment. As he walked down the long corridor to her room, he thought about what would happen to her once she was released. She'll be all right, he told himself. She could stay in one of the shelters until her memory returned or one of the social services agencies made other arrangements. She's not my problem, he reminded himself as he walked into her room.

She stood at the window, her back to him, apparently unaware of his presence. For a moment, he simply looked at her, unable to help but notice how the morning sunshine shone not only through the window, but also through her thin cotton gown. He could see the darker lines of her figure, the slight whisper of her waist, the thin hips.

He also noticed her posture... defenseless, vulnerable, her forehead resting against the window as if it were the glass itself that held her upright.

"Jane?"

She turned around and immediately straightened, her lips curving into a smile of pleasure. "Hi, Dr. Longford." She moved away from the window and sat down on the edge of the bed. Her green eyes focused on him expectantly.

"Are you feeling better this morning?" he asked.

She nodded. "My headache is gone, I feel much stronger. There's only this one slight problem..." She smiled wryly. "I seem to have misplaced my mind."

He returned her smile, having recognized over the past two days that she hid her fear, her uncertainty, beneath a wry sense of humor. "No memories after the police told you your name?"

Her smile wavered slightly, speaking more than anything she could say verbally.

"It will come," he quickly assured her, wanting to see the sunshine of her smile once again. "However, we've gone through the test results and we've come to the conclusion that there's no physiological reason for your amnesia." He hesitated, then continued. "Dr. Waylon is of the opinion that perhaps your amnesia is due to some sort of psychological trauma."

"That's the good news? That you've come to the conclusion that I'm crazy?"

He laughed. "No, Jane. Nobody thinks you're crazy. But it's possible that, for some reason, your mind has shut itself down." She looked at him blankly. "It's sort of like a computer. The files to your memory are all in there, but for some reason, you can't access them."

"So what happens now?"

"I recommend that you make an appointment to talk to a therapist. But this isn't the news I really came to deliver. The good news is that Dr. Waylon is releasing you this afternoon."

"Release? Oh, how nice." Only the slight trembling of her lower lip told him of her distress at the thought of leaving the hospital.

"Jane," he said softly as he joined her on the edge of the bed. He picked up one of her hands in his. "I can imagine how frightening the thought of leaving the hospital is, but there's nothing more we can do for you here."

She jerked her hand out of his and jumped off the bed, her eyes flashing emerald fires as she glared at him. "How can you imagine how frightening it is for me? You know who you are. When you leave here, you'll go to your home, where you have all your things surrounding you. All I have to do is figure out where I'm going from here...who the hell Jane Smith really is." Her eyes misted. "God, I don't know who I am...I don't know anything about me."

She crumbled before him, the fire of anger in her eyes extinguished by the tears that filled their bright green depths. "I'm sorry," she whispered. "I didn't mean to yell at you."

"It's all right. I'd say you've got a right to be angry."

She nodded and tears began to slip down her cheeks. Before Frank could say anything else, she sank back down on the bed, covered her eyes and sobbed.

Frank hesitated only a moment, then, feeling awkward and helpless, he placed an arm around her shoulder in an attempt to soothe her. She turned her face into his lab jacket and shook with the intensity of her tears.

Her body was warm against his, and she smelled of soap and shampoo. He murmured meaningless platitudes, waiting patiently for her to cry herself out.

When finally her sobs had dissipated to occasional hiccups, he moved away from her and handed her a tissue. "Feel better?" he asked.

"A little," she admitted. "And more than a bit embarrassed," she added, wringing the tissue in her hands.

"No need to be embarrassed. I'd say you earned the right to a good cry. Sometimes it's the best medicine."

"I don't like to cry. I think the last time I did was when I was twelve years old and my dog got hit by a car." The minute the words left her lips, she looked at him in amazement. "My God . . . I remember that. I remember the dog was a poodle . . . a black toy poodle and his name was . . . was . . ." She frowned as again a blankness descended over her mind. She looked at Frank in frustration. "It's gone. The memory was there—so vivid, so clear, but now it's gone."

"That's great," he said, reaching out and gently tucking a strand of her hair behind her ear. "It's a beginning. That's the way it's probably going to come back. Piece by piece, and before you know it, you'll remember all of it."

"But how long will it take?"

"I can't answer that. Nobody can. It's completely unpredictable."

She nodded, straightening her shoulders. "Then I guess I'll just have to take this one day at a time," she said, smiling at him with a burst of bravado. "I don't suppose you know if there are any job openings here at the hospital...something that pays in room and board?"

He shook his head. "But Dr. Waylon contacted Social Services to see if we can find you a place to stay. We're not going to let you walk out of here with no place to go." He stood up from the bed, his gaze caught by the suitcase of clothing the police had retrieved from the rental cottage. "At least you have some of your own clothing."

She nodded absently, then frowned. "You think it's possible the police might have missed something in that room?"

"Like what?"

"Oh, I don't know...a slip of paper, a keepsake...something that might jiggle the memories back into my head. Surely there would be something in that room that would tell me *something*." She seemed to warm to the idea. "Can you give me directions to these cabins? I'll go there as soon as I get out of here." She looked at him eagerly.

"I'll tell you what. I get out of here at three o'clock this afternoon. Why don't you let me take you out there," Frank suggested.

She looked at him hesitantly. "Are you sure you wouldn't mind? I don't want to impose on your time."

Frank smiled at her. "I wouldn't have offered if it were an imposition. Besides, if nothing definite pans out there, I can take you to wherever Social Services sets you up to stay." He stood up. "So it's settled. Dr. Waylon will see to your release and I'll be here to pick you up at three o'clock this afternoon." With a final smile, he left the room, immediately bumping into Russ in the corridor.

"Did you tell her she was going to be released?" Russ asked.

"Yeah, I told her. Did you talk to Social Services?"

Russ nodded. "They're supposed to get back to me some time in the next couple of hours."

"Let me know what they work out. I made arrangements to take her wherever she needs to go when I get off work at three." With a backward wave, Frank headed down the hallway for the rest of his morning rounds.

She stood at the window and looked out into the world she was about to enter...a world that seemed strange and somehow threatening. She had a name, but it felt wrong, as though it didn't belong to her. Jane Smith. It told her nothing of herself. She had nothing else to go with the name...no past, no idea of Jane Smith's favorite foods, her personal likes and dislikes.

"Jane Smith. I'm Jane Smith." She said the name out loud over and over again, as if by mere repetition she could finally claim the name as her own.

And now, she stood waiting for a man she barely knew, but instinctively trusted, to take her out into an alien world. "What a mess," she mumbled, turning away from the window with a sigh.

That morning, she had awakened with the hope that somehow, during the night while she'd slept, her memory had miraculously been restored to her. But miracles seemed to be in short supply and she'd awakened with the same damnable blackness obscuring her brain.

"Jane?"

She looked up to see Dr. Longford standing in the doorway. "Hi," she said, relieved that he'd actually come for her. At the moment, he seemed the only thing she could depend on, the only anchor in a storm-tossed sea.

"All ready?" he asked.

She nodded and he disappeared out the door, only to return pushing a wheelchair. "That's really not necessary," she protested.

"Ah, we always have our guests leave our facility in style," he said, gesturing for her to have a seat.

"I feel ridiculous," she said as he pushed her down the corridor toward the front exit.

"You don't look ridiculous," he countered.

As they passed the receptionist's desk, she was suddenly struck by the magnitude of her position. "What about my bill? I don't know if I have insurance...."

"Don't worry about it now. They've put everything on an account and you can deal with it once you know who you are and what the situation is."

As they passed out the exit door of the hospital, a woman carrying a baby hurried in. Do I have a family? Jane wondered wildly. Is there a little girl or boy crying someplace because their mommy is lost? And if there *was* a child, was there a man? A husband?

She looked down at her hands. No rings, not a single sign that a wedding band had ever rested on her finger. Maybe I'm the type who didn't need to wear a symbol of commitment, she thought. She immediately dismissed the idea, instinctively knowing that she was the type who would wear a wedding ring proudly.

No, she felt sure in her heart there were no children, just as there was no husband, no family to mourn her, to report her disappearance from their world. Again she felt an enormous isolation, a deep sense of aloneness. Where did she fit? Where did she belong?

"Jane, are you all right?"

She resurfaced from her thoughts to see Frank's brown eyes looking at her in concern. She realized they were at the curb, where a bright red sports car awaited them. "I'm fine," she assured him.

Within moments, she was in the passenger seat and he was steering the car away from the hospital. The windows were down, letting in warm, salt-scented air and whipping Jane's hair into disarray.

As they drove through the heart of the small town of Garett Beach, she looked out the window with interest, waiting for something, anything, to ring a bell of familiarity. But nothing did. It was as if she saw the cozy coastal town for the very first time. She sighed.

"That was an awfully big sigh. Are you sure you're all right?" Frank asked.

She nodded. "Just disappointed. I'd hoped seeing the area might jog a memory or two. But there's nothing."

He reached across the seat and lightly touched her hand. "Don't expect too much from yourself. I have a feeling the harder you try, the fewer the results." He released her hand and refocused his attention on his driving.

Jane was grateful it had been Dr. Frank Longford who'd found her on the beach. She was aware that he was going above and beyond the call of duty by chauffeuring her around.

She now looked at him, noting the way his thick dark hair waved slightly along the nape of his neck, the sensual fullness of his lower lip, the strong jawline that spoke of inner strength and character. She'd been so caught up in her own personal drama she hadn't really noticed that he was an incredibly handsome man. "Is there a Mrs. Longford?" she asked suddenly.

He shook his head. "No, I'm not married. I almost was once, but it was a very long time ago."

There was something in his tone that made her think it was a subject he didn't want to talk about. "I've decided I'm not married, either," she said, once again looking down at her hands. "It doesn't look like I've

ever worn a ring." She looked back out the window.
"But I guess I'll know who I am when we get to these
cabins. There has to be something there that will shake
up the stubborn hiding memories."

As they left the town behind, they traveled a road
that carried them along the ocean shore. The waves
rolled, sparkling in splendor as the sun kissed each
one. "This is beautiful. Have you always lived here?"

"Born and raised right here in Garett Beach. I left
town long enough to complete medical school, then
returned and bought the house where I live now."

"Do your parents still live here?" she asked, immediately wondering about her own. Where were her
parents? Were they worried about her?

"No, my parents passed away several years ago," he
answered, pulling into the parking area near a group
of small, ramshackle cabins.

"This is where I was staying?" Jane looked at the
cabins in dismay. She couldn't imagine actually making a conscious decision to stay in such a place. What
set of circumstances could possibly have provoked her
into staying in such a horrible place?

"The police said you were registered to cabin six.
The owner recognized you from the Polaroid they
took of you." He shut off the engine and turned to
her. "My place is over there." He pointed down the
beach, where, in the distance, she could see a house
with a large back porch. "I saw you each evening
walking on the beach. You always walked after dark,
and you were always alone."

Jane looked at the isolated stretch of beach, trying to remember what might have driven her to walk it by herself at night. Her headache made an encore appearance, pounding with a dull intensity across her forehead and at the base of her head.

Together they got out of the car and approached the cabin where an Office sign hung askew. Before they got to the door, a large man in a stained T-shirt came out.

"Figured you'd be back. The cops were here earlier this morning." He scratched the side of his protruding belly, cocking his head to one side. He immediately reminded Jane of a big, scruffy dog, scratching at fleas while he eyed something curiously. "You really got that amnesia stuff?"

Dr. Longford moved closer to her and placed an arm lightly on her shoulder. She welcomed the warmth of his support. "Ms. Smith has had an accident and is just experiencing a little disorientation. We'd like to take a look around the cabin, see if the police gathered up all her possessions. Could you let her in?" Frank asked.

The man shrugged his massive shoulders and pulled a key ring from his pants pocket. "I suppose it won't hurt nothing," he agreed, his gaze lingering on Jane as he handed her the key. "I never knew anyone who had real amnesia...although my wife sure enough tries to forget she's married to me."

Jane forced a smile, the key burning urgently into her palm. She hoped it would be the key that would open up her memory.

Cabin six was at the very end of the row of faded, neglected-looking small buildings.

"I can't believe I was staying here," Jane whispered, appalled when she stepped inside the tiny structure. She looked around distastefully. The interior of the place smelled of mildew and age and hopelessness. The sparse furniture was old and cigarette-scarred.

The kitchen area was even more dismal, the stove was grease-splattered, the sink brown with rusty water stains and the apartment-size refrigerator hummed loudly, discordantly.

"I don't know anything about myself, but I just can't understand why I would stay in such a horrid place." She walked over to the closet and stared at the wire hangers inside.

She was conscious of Dr. Longford standing in the doorway, watching as she opened drawers, looking for something, anything, that the police might have missed. But there was nothing. She sank down on the edge of the bed in defeat.

She had hoped that by merely walking into the cabin, a light bulb would go off in her head and all the recollections of her life would come tumbling back to her. "What happened to me?" She stared at Frank in despair. "Who am I? Who is Jane Smith? It's like I have no past. What was I doing in a place like this?"

"I don't know, but one thing is damn sure. There's nothing here for you. Let's get out of here." He walked over to where she sat on the bed and held out his hand. "We'll go to my place and call Dr. Waylon and see what he heard from Social Services."

"Are ... are you sure?"

He nodded, surprised as she threw her arms around his neck. "Thank you," she whispered against his throat, her sweet clean scent surrounding him.

Minutes later as they drove to Frank's house, he caught himself casting her surreptitious glances. From the moment he'd found her on his beach, he'd tried to keep his thoughts purely those of a doctor to a patient.

But, remembering the heat of her breath against his neck, the feel of her body heat momentarily against his, he found his thoughts distinctly undoctorlike.

Where had she come from? Where had she been? What was it she had said? That it was as if she had fallen from the sky, a woman without a past, a woman whose future seemed uncertain. A very attractive woman.

He tightened his grip on the steering wheel and focused his attention back on the road. He was a solitary man. He was a busy doctor with an overload of patients. It didn't matter how attractive she was, he had no time, no place in his life for a woman.

Besides, the very last thing he would ever do was allow himself to get involved in a relationship with a woman without memories. He'd tried it once ... with a woman who'd refused to share her memories, and the result had been tragic. He was far too smart to repeat past errors.

He'd take Jane to his house and they'd call Russ. Then he'd drop Jane off at whatever place Social Services had arranged and that would be the end of it. She would be taken care of and eventually she would be all right.

Confident that he had it all under control, he turned into his driveway. He'd be a Good Samaritan and do what he could to help her, but he wasn't about to be a fool and ruin the peaceful, solitary existence he'd made for himself.

Chapter 3

They were greeted at Frank's door by two big dogs barking and jumping in excitement at their arrival. "They don't bite," Frank assured her as she hesitated on the front porch and eyed them in distrust. "They're far too dumb to bite," he added wryly.

He pushed the front door open wider to allow her entry.

She stepped in, laughing as the two dogs jumped at her, licking at the air as they attempted to lavish kisses on her face. "Oh, they're darling," she exclaimed, patting first one, then the other.

"Mutt...Jeff...down," Frank commanded. The dogs immediately obeyed, both flopping on the floor, their backsides still quivering in rapture.

The dogs' silly antics released some of her pent-up emotion and again Jane laughed. "They're so sweet," she said as she crouched down to scratch first one dog, then the other behind their furry ears.

"They're a pain in the butt," Frank returned with an affectionate grin at the two dogs. "Well—" he looked at her awkwardly "—how about a cup of coffee?"

"Sure, if it's not too much trouble."

"No trouble. I'll just go put a pot on." He looked around the living room and grimaced slightly. "Just ignore the mess and make yourself at home. I'll be right back."

When he was gone, she looked around with interest. Decorated in southwestern colors, the room was spacious yet informal. It embraced her with its air of comfort and homeyness. A stone fireplace occupied one wall, holding the remaining ashes of a fire from some distant time. The morning newspaper was spread out on the wooden coffee table, a dirty mug sitting atop the open pages.

It was a place to live in, the furniture comfortable and rather worn. It was also a place obviously belonging to a man alone. There was no hint of a woman's touch, a feminine hand in the decor, and it held the air of slight neglect. A light cover of dust veiled the beauty of the wood of the coffee tables. Records and CDs littered the top of the stereo system, as if ignoring the storage space where they belonged.

As she walked around the room, the dogs followed behind her, their tails wagging like metronome pendulums keeping time to an inaudible tune.

She moved toward the large sliding glass door, catching her breath as she peered outside. The beach stretched out before her, sandy and white, and beyond that the ocean glittered orange and pink, borrowing the colors of the setting sun. The scene offered a sensation of tranquility—peace—momentarily assuaging the anxiety that gnawed at her.

"Cream or sugar?" Frank called from the kitchen.

"No, just black," she answered absently, her attention still captured by the serene landscape before her. The brilliantly colored sails of a boat appeared on the horizon, silhouetted against the sinking ball of fire the sun had become.

Do I like to sail? Do I like the water? She turned the questions over in her head, frustrated with her inability to answer the most mundane of queries about herself. Why was I staying in those cabins? Why don't I have a driver's license, any sort of official identification?

She leaned her head against the warm pane of the glass, trying to recapture the momentary sense of peace she'd felt when she'd first gazed out the window. But it was gone, usurped by the uncertainty that gripped her and kept her a prisoner to the blankness of her mind.

"Here you go," Frank spoke from behind her.

She turned and accepted the cup of coffee from him with a grateful smile. "You've got a beautiful view," she said, gesturing out the door.

He nodded as he unlocked the sliding glass door and opened it. "Come on, let's have our coffee out here. The boys usually take an evening run."

At the sound of the word *run* two pairs of ears pricked up and the dogs barked their eagerness. They zoomed past Jane, through the opening, across the patio and hit the beach, barking their joy at the sudden freedom.

"They have no manners whatsoever," Frank observed wryly, moving aside to allow her to exit the house before him.

She stepped out onto the wooden patio, the sound of the ocean now audible. Like the noise of a mother's heartbeat to a baby in the womb, the rhythmic whooshing of the waves as they claimed the shore was reassuring, comforting.

She leaned against the wooden railing that surrounded the patio and sipped her coffee, her gaze going back to the sailboat in the distance, then to the two dogs romping playfully in the sand.

The warmth of the evening embraced her, and in the distance she could hear the melodic sound of wind chimes singing to the soft evening breeze that whispered off the water. "It's so peaceful here," she said, almost reluctant to break nature's noise with the intrusive sound of her voice.

"Hmm, that's what keeps me here," Frank said from where he sat on one of the deck chairs. "There are days when I think it's time to make a change, find a new place to live, then I take a few minutes and sit out here and realize I must be crazy to even consider giving all this up."

"And you can't be crazy...I'm the crazy one here." She smiled, but felt one corner of her lip tremble uncontrollably, once again overwhelmed by her circumstances.

"Not crazy," he corrected firmly. "Just momentarily confused."

This time her smile was genuine, grateful. "So what do we do now?" she asked.

Frank shrugged. "I called Dr. Waylon while I was in the kitchen and he gave me the address of the shelter you can go to. It's in Wilmington, which is about a forty-five-minute ride from here. But there's no hurry. Enjoy your coffee and relax for a few minutes."

She nodded. She would face the uncertainty of the shelter when she got there. For now, she just wanted to breath in the sweet-scented air, enjoy the awesome glory of the scenery that for the moment made her loss of memory seem like an insignificant annoyance.

"You make a good cup of coffee," she commented as she took another sip of the fragrant brew. She grinned wryly. "The best I can remember."

He raised his dark eyebrows and smiled, acknowledging her black humor. "Learning to make decent coffee was a necessity. I had to learn to brew a good pot to take the taste of the hospital sludge I drink all day out of my mouth. I also make a pretty mean omelet. Are you hungry?'' he asked.

"A little," she admitted, then grinned. "Your hospital-sludge coffee can't be as bad as some of the food I was served there."

"That bad, huh?"

"That bad."

He stood up and raised two fingers to his lips. With a deep breath he emitted a loud whistle that stopped the two dogs dead in their tracks and sent them running back toward the house.

"I always wished I could do that," Jane said. "I had a neighbor-boy who used to whistle like that all the time and he tried and tried to teach me, but I never did get the hang of it." For a moment, her head was filled with the picture of the boy, a husky redhead with freckles and big brown eyes. What was his name?

The image of his face shimmered in her brain. She closed her eyes, mentally reaching to embrace it, but as she did, it flitted away, leaving behind only the dark emptiness she'd come to expect.

"Damn." She sighed, opening her eyes to see Frank studying her. "It's so frustrating. Bits and pieces tease me, then disappear."

"Don't be too hard on yourself. It's a good sign that you're remembering anything at all." Frank opened the back door to allow the dogs inside, then gestured her in.

He led her through the living room and to the kitchen. "Have a seat and make yourself at home.

After I feed these hungry mutts, I can get to work on our omelet extraordinaire.''

Jane sat down at the glass-topped table and watched as he filled two big bowls full of dried dog food, then set them down on the floor. The two dogs attacked the food as if they hadn't eaten in months. "Are they always so enthusiastic?" she asked, laughing as one of the dogs finished the food and proceeded to use his nose to shove the bowl back in Frank's direction.

"Only about food," he replied as he placed more of the hard chunks in the bowl. "They're actually pretty intelligent, especially where food is concerned, but they become terribly stupid when I tell them to do something they don't want to do, like go outside on a rainy day."

Jane laughed again as both dogs looked up at him as if to protest his observation about their mental capacity. "How long have you had them?"

"I found them on the beach a little over a year ago. They were just puppies, bundled together in a gunnysack, apparently abandoned and left to drown. Thank God I spotted them before the tide came in."

"You seem to make a habit of finding things on the beach."

"Hmm, dogs, seashells, pieces of driftwood, beautiful women.... Living on the beach is never dull." He opened the refrigerator door and gathered together the ingredients for the omelet. The dogs finished eating and lay down beneath the table near Jane's feet.

She felt a slight warmth rush through her as she thought of what he'd said. Beautiful women.... Was she beautiful? Her hand reached up and touched the side of her neck, the area where the scar slightly puckered her skin. She knew it wasn't visible above the collar of her blouse, but she knew it was there. She also knew that he had seen it, but he hadn't asked her about it, hadn't mentioned it at all.

Over the past twenty-four hours, she had spent long minutes in front of a mirror, studying the face that stared back at her. Yes, she supposed it was a pretty face. But it seemed unrelated, having little to do with her. She didn't feel beautiful on the inside. She simply felt confused.

She refocused her attention on Frank and watched him as he worked at the stove. He moved with a familiar grace around the kitchen. It was easy to tell he was a man accustomed to taking care of himself. "Green peppers, onions, mushrooms and cheese okay?" he asked.

"Sounds wonderful. The least you can do is let me chop the onions and peppers." She got up from the table and moved to stand next to him. She took the knife he offered her and began chopping up the vegetables.

As they worked side by side, a strained silence descended between them. Jane chopped slowly, methodically, her mind whirling as she tried to think of something to say to fill the silence.

She understood his reluctance to speak, knew it would be difficult to carry on any kind of discussion with a woman who knew nothing about herself. Her lack of identity frustrated even the most simple questions, discouraged the social interaction of getting to know each other.

"Do you like being a doctor?" she asked, knowing the question was rather lame, but desperate to start a conversation about anything that would keep her mind off the emptiness inside her.

"I don't remember a time when I wanted to do anything else," he answered as he broke eggs into a bowl and whisked them briskly with a fork. "My mom used to tell me that when all the other kids were playing at being army men, I was always the medic. When they were playing cowboys and Indians, I was the medicine man."

Jane smiled, imagining him with his face painted in brilliant streaks, a feather nodding atop his dark hair, his face solemn as he healed his fellow braves. "So you had a good childhood."

"As good as any." Then, as if sensing her need, he continued. "I grew up in a house not far from here. My father taught school and my mother was a paralegal." He stared ahead reflectively. "The beach and the ocean were as much a part of my life as anything."

"Garett Beach doesn't seem to be much of a tourist town," she observed, remembering the drive through the small downtown area as they'd left the hospital.

"We've been lucky. The tourists haven't found us. They seem to prefer the beaches north of here, like Myrtle Beach." He paused a moment to add the chopped peppers and onions to the pan. "Garett Beach will probably always be just what it is now . . . a small beachfront community where everyone knows everyone else's business." He grinned at her. "Peyton Place on the water." He plugged in a shiny toaster and set in two pieces of bread to brown.

"Then obviously I don't come from here. If I did, everyone in town could tell me who I am and what I'm like." The toast popped up, as he reached for it, and she waved him away, buttering it herself and placing two more pieces in the toaster.

"No, but you might come from another small town where somebody will be able to fill in the blanks of who you are." He smiled at her confidently. "The police will continue to check missing persons files. I'm sure it's just a matter of time before somebody comes forward who knows you." He took the omelet pan off the burner. "And in the meantime, you might re-member everything on your own."

"I hope so," she said fervently.

As they sat down to eat, Frank found his gaze studying her, not clinically as a doctor, but with the curiosity of a man. She was beautiful, there was no question about that. But it was a haunting beauty. Something in her eyes spoke of dark secrets, shadowy depths unexplored, mysterious green eyes with a hint of pain.

He forced his gaze away. Of course there were dark secrets there. The woman had amnesia. Her very sense of identity was a mystery at the moment; even she didn't know what painful memories might be hidden in the recesses of her mind. He thought of the night he'd rushed her to the hospital, that single moment when her eyes had opened, dazed and murky but holding a plea so intense it had reached inside and squeezed his heart.

He dismissed these thoughts from his mind and rubbed his forehead tiredly. As usual, it had been a long day and obviously his overtiredness was making him more than a little bit imaginative. Whatever he'd thought he'd seen in Jane's eyes that night was surely just her reaction to waking up momentarily and being afraid, displaced, uncertain as to where she was and what had happened to her.

"Mmm, this tastes so good," she said, effectively pulling him from his reverie.

"Better than the hospital food?" he asked teasingly.

"No comparison. What I can't figure out is how institutional cooking can make pork, eggs, cheese and poultry all taste exactly the same."

He laughed, again pleased that even though she had no memory, she did have a sense of humor. "More toast?" he asked.

"Oh, no." She shoved her empty plate aside. "I couldn't eat another bite." She sipped her coffee, then looked at him curiously. "So, I guess we'd better get me to that shelter."

Frank nodded, suddenly reluctant as he thought of her living in one of the shelters that offered safety to the homeless, the abused, the hopeless. They were dismal places...places where people came when there was no place else to turn...places for people who had nobody else who cared about them.

He looked at her once again, noting her frailty, the air of vulnerability that clung to her like a shawl. "You know, I've been thinking lately of hiring a house-keeper. I hadn't thought of a live-in situation, but I do have an extra bedroom. If you'd like..."

"I'd love to," she answered before he had a chance to finish. Her frown creased her forehead and her eyes darkened to a muddied green. "I'd really rather stay here than at a shelter. I promise I'll work hard. I'll have this place sparkling from top to bottom." She broke off with a flush, then continued less fervently. "I think, more than anything, I hate this feeling of helplessness, of having absolutely no resources and being so dependent. If I could stay here and actually work, I'd feel so much better."

"Everyone needs a little help in their lives now and then. Right now, it's your turn. Besides, this way we're both getting something. You feel better and I get my house cleaned."

He heard the hopelessness in her sigh. "I just wish I could reach inside and shake out all the blackness in my head."

He reached across the table and took one of her hands in his, an unexpected spark of energy coursing through it as she returned his grip. "Don't push too hard. Sometimes the harder you push, the more elusive memories become." He released her hand immediately, uncomfortable with the evocative pleasantness of her warm grasp. It unsettled him.

They cleared off the table and stacked the dishes in the dishwasher, then went outside onto the patio, where night had fallen and the moon sparkled its reflective light on the water. Although the day had been hot, a cool breeze blew off the water.

Frank resumed his position in a deck chair, while Jane stood against the railing, offering him a perfect view of her moonlit profile.

He sighed tiredly as he leaned back and closed his eyes, shutting out her attractiveness. From where he sat, he could smell her subtle perfume, feel the restless energy and frustration that emanated from her.

It felt strange to be sharing his private space with somebody else. It had been a very long time since he'd invited anyone into his personal domain. Not since... He shoved the thought away before it could completely form in his mind. He refused to be drawn into painful memories of the past.

He looked back at Jane. Maybe there was something to be said for losing one's memory. At least that way there was no heartache connected with remembrances of the past. Yet, he knew the painful memories were as important as the happy ones. Past experiences were what made people who they were, the past was what gave a person their heart, their soul.

And what kind of soul did this woman have? Where had she come from and what experiences had brought her to his beach? He wasn't sure he wanted to know.

He'd long ago realized that he was destined to live alone, to use his energy to heal the sick, mend the broken. That was exactly what he would do with Jane. He'd heal her broken wings and send her back to whatever life she'd forgotten. He didn't want to know her heart or her soul. Someplace she had a life . . . possibly a special man waiting for her return.

Now he stood up and stretched with his arms overhead, the long hours of the day creating an overwhelming exhaustion. "I hate to be a poor host, but I'm really beat. If you don't mind, I'll show you to the guest room, then I'll call it a night."

"That's fine," she replied. "Actually, I'm pretty tired myself."

Together they went back into the house. Frank grabbed her small bag, which he'd dropped earlier just inside the front door, then showed her to the guest bedroom.

The room was small, sparsely furnished with a single bed and a chest of drawers, but the window offered a beautiful view of the beach.

"It's not much," he said, for the first time noticing the austerity of the room.

"It's fine," she assured him. "Besides, you'll never know how much I appreciate your hospitality, Dr. Longford."

Again he felt a moment of strange discomfort as her green eyes gazed at him gratefully. "No problem, and you can drop the formality. Just call me Frank," he said, setting her bag inside the doorway. "I'm right next door if you need anything."

"I'm sure I'll be fine."

He started to leave, but hesitated as she called his name softly. He turned back.

"Thank you, Frank . . . for everything." Her eyes were luminous, shining like brilliant gemstones, and for just a moment, Frank wondered if they would shine in that same beautiful fashion if he kissed her.

He nodded and fled from the room, appalled by his thoughts. He had no intention of kissing Jane, no intention of getting personally involved with her at all. He'd only offered her the job because he couldn't stand the thought of her being in a shelter. And besides, he had been meaning to hire a housekeeper. He was usually too tired after the long hours at the hospital to worry about cleaning. The situation would work to both their advantages.

Now, if he could just ignore the coil of heat that wrapped inside him as he went into his own bedroom....

Heat. It surrounded her, engulfed her. She was drowning in it, choking in it. Each deep breath she took scorched her lungs, stung her eyes.

Fire. She could hear it crackling, sizzling. The noise filled her with stark terror. She stood in a small, enclosed area, a place she didn't recognize. Around her, smoke billowed like black clouds, obscuring her vision, causing her to choke as she gasped deep breaths of searing heat.

Above the sound of the fire's fury she heard the distant, mournful wail of a baby. Panic gripped her, choking her as thickly as the smoke. She had to...she had to do something...something important. She had to get away, escape. She was losing her mind....

The baby...something about the baby filled her with horror, with a dread too great to bear. She needed to run, but couldn't, was frozen in place. The baby's cries rose and fell, and she placed her hands over her ears, not wanting to hear them anymore.

She smelled death in the air, a scent that burned her nose and made her stomach churn. Death surrounded her, and she somehow knew it was all her fault.

She gripped her hands together, surprised to feel them slick and sticky. As if from a great distance, she looked down at them. Blood. Bright red blood covered both her hands. Smoke swirled like a black mist, and in the mist images flashed one after another... bright red blood, horrifying death cries, searing flames.

Jane bolted up in bed, gasping for breath, her body covered in a fine sheen of perspiration. She slapped a hand over her pounding heart and stared around the darkness, trying to orient herself.

Moonlight spilled into the window and painted the room in a soft silvery glow, and she instantly recognized where she was. Yes, of course, she was in Frank's spare bedroom. She was safe here.

She released a shuddery breath, the images of her dream still vivid enough to cause a choking nausea to crawl up the back of her throat.

On trembling legs she left the small bed and walked over to the window. She raised it high to let in the pungent ocean air, hoping it would blow away the memory of her horrible nightmare. The cool air caused goose bumps to dance across the surface of her damp skin, but it did nothing to diffuse the strength of her nightmare.

She stared out at the expanse of moonlit beach, striving for the serenity it had offered her earlier. She reached for some of its tranquility to soothe the anxiety that gnawed insidiously at her insides.

But as she remembered the images from the dream, as those horrid visions danced in her brain, there was no modicum of peace to be found. *My fault,* some inner voice screamed in her head. *It's all my fault.*

Nightmare . . . had it been a dream or was it a memory? Her heart resumed its erratic beating at this thought. If it had been a nightmare, then what demons had driven her to dream such a thing?

And if it had been a memory . . . then who exactly was she, and worse . . . what had she done?

Chapter 4

"Good morning," Jane greeted Frank as he approached the kitchen. She'd heard his alarm go off earlier, then the sounds of the shower running and had been expecting him.

"Morning," he replied, hesitating in the doorway, obviously surprised to see her already there. "You're up early."

"I didn't sleep very well. I hope you don't mind...I made coffee."

"Believe me, I don't mind." He moved over to the cabinet and grabbed a cup. "The longest moments of the day are those in the morning when you have to wait for the first pot of coffee to drip through." He poured himself a cup, took a sip, then sank down at the table, his gaze curious as it lingered on her. "So, what was the problem? The room too hot, too cold? The bed too lumpy?''

She shook her head, noting how handsome he looked in his white shirt and navy slacks. "No, everything was fine. I was quite comfortable. I just had a night of bad dreams," she confessed, frowning as she once again thought of the frightening visions that had haunted her sleep.

He wrapped his hands around his coffee mug. "Want to talk about it?" he asked.

"There's really nothing to talk about. The dreams were just disjointed confusing images. Nothing made any sense at all." She turned away from him and gazed out the window, unwilling to share the details of the disturbing night.

"It was probably just a reflection of the confused state of your mind. You've been under quite a lot of stress in the past couple of days."

"Yes . . . yes I'm sure that's it." She grabbed on to the rational explanation like a drowning woman clinging to a life preserver. Surely that was what it had been . . . the crazy dreams of a woman struggling to come to terms with the uncertainty of her life. It had nothing to do with her past or any real memories.

She joined him at the table, putting the haunting nightmares behind her. "How did you sleep?"

"Like a log, but I always do." He looked at his watch. "I'm going to run down to the hospital. There are a couple of patients I want to check on." He stood up and drained his coffee. "I'll be back here around quarter to nine, and I think we should get you over to the courthouse. We can tell Social Services about our working arrangement and see what other help they might be able to offer you.''

"Are you sure you don't mind?" She looked at him worriedly, again hating the dependency she'd developed for this man who was a relative stranger.

"Jane, I said I didn't mind and I don't. Just make yourself at home while I'm gone and I'll see you in a couple of hours." The dogs followed him out of the kitchen and to the front door.

She knew he'd left when the dogs returned to the kitchen, resuming their sleeping positions beneath the table. Jane got up and went over to the window, staring out at the dawn just breaking over the water.

A new day, but she was no closer to knowing anything about herself than she had been the night before. Every morning she awakened with the hope that somehow in the night her memory had been miraculously restored.

She turned away from the window, looking at the wall clock hanging above the stove. Seven o'clock, and Frank would be back here in less than two hours.

She needed a shower. Hopefully, it would successfully wash away the lingering unease brought on by the nightmares.

Minutes later, as she stood beneath the hot water, she found her thoughts drifting to Dr. Longford. Frank. Somehow, in thinking of him as Frank rather than Dr. Longford, she instantly got a mental vision of the man, rather than the physician.

While she'd spent time with him in the hospital setting, she hadn't seen much beyond his white doctor's jacket and competent manner. But since then, especially this morning, she had seen him simply as a very attractive man.

She wondered why he wasn't married. Surely a good-looking doctor would be considered a real catch among the single women of Garett Beach. "But perhaps this is one handsome fish who doesn't want to get caught," she murmured to herself. But why?

She shoved these thoughts aside. She had enough to worry about in figuring out who she was. She didn't need to expend any additional energy trying to figure out the inner workings of Frank Longford.

Still, what would she have done without him? Where would she be at this moment had he not offered her his hospitality and a job as his housekeeper? The question sent a shiver of revulsion up her spine as she remembered the horrible rental cottage. Why had she been staying there? she asked herself again. What might have possibly gone wrong with her life that would have forced her to be living in such a place?

She sighed and shoved the questions out of her mind. She thought perhaps Frank was right. The harder she pushed to recapture her past, the more elusive it became.

Although Social Services certainly couldn't give her back her memory, they could at least arrange support of some kind, perhaps a few resources she could access to discover exactly who Jane Smith was.

She was feeling quite optimistic by the time Frank arrived back at the house.

"All ready?" he asked when she greeted him at the front door.

"How were your patients?" she asked once they were driving toward town.

He looked at her in surprise, as if he wasn't accustomed to somebody asking him about his work. "Fine, although I need to be back at the hospital by noon. I've got a tonsillectomy scheduled for a very frightened little six-year-old."

"Surely we'll be finished long before then," Jane said.

"We'll just have to see how it goes," he replied.

They fell into silence. This time, it wasn't strained as it had been the night before; rather, it was a companionable one, broken from time to time by Frank indicating points of interest along the way.

Jane viewed their surroundings with pleasure. She'd been too caught up in her own personal drama the night before to really see the area when they'd first driven out to Frank's house.

Frank's home was set on an isolated stretch of beach, the nearest neighbor the rental cottages in the far distance. As they approached the town of Garett Beach, he pointed out an ancient abandoned lighthouse on an outcrop of rocks, a restaurant that served the best steamed crabs in the area, a house that was reputed to be haunted.

The Garett Beach Courthouse was a stately three story building in the center of the town square. They found the department they wanted on the third floor.

Jane flushed slightly as Frank explained the situation to the woman behind the desk. The woman eyed her as if Jane were a scientific experiment gone awry.

"Fill out these papers and bring them back to me," the woman said as she handed Jane a sheath of printed forms attached to a clipboard.

Frank guided her to one of the plastic chairs and handed her a pen from his pocket. Jane stared down at the first form and heaved a deep sigh.

"What's the matter?" Frank whispered, the scent of his pleasant cologne surrounding her as he leaned toward her.

Jane showed him the questions on the first three lines. "Name, address and phone number. How am I supposed to answer these? I can fill in my name...but I'm trying to discover everything else."

Frank's jaw muscles clenched in aggravation. "Apparently your dilemma wasn't understood." He took the papers from her and once again approached the woman at the desk.

It was nearly eleven when they finally left the courthouse, Frank fuming over the frustrating red tape and Jane silent in defeat.

He shot a sideways look at her. She looked so small, so lost. A surge of anger swept through him as he thought of the way she had been treated by those who were supposed to be in the position to help. They had eyed her suspiciously, with a slight edge of contempt, as if somehow she had brought on her condition herself, or had been infected with a dread social disease.

"At least you have a place to stay and a job that will give you some spending money," he offered. "And surely the police will be able to discover something."

She nodded, her gaze not wavering from the landscape outside. Frank noted the way the sunshine that streamed in through the car window caressed the delicate features of her face. With the natural light stroking the dark richness of her hair and illuminating the green depths of her eyes, Frank felt a sudden sharp unexpected twinge of desire.

He stared back at the road, irritated by the swift appearance of the unwanted emotion. For the rest of the drive to his place, he was silent, focusing all his attention on the physical act of driving. He didn't want to analyze the negative sentiment, he didn't even want to acknowledge it. He simply wanted it to go away and never return.

When they got back to his house, he dropped her off, then proceeded to the hospital, his thoughts still sending warnings to his heart.

Surely we can share the same house and not become personally involved, he reasoned. Granted, he was attracted to her, but he'd been attracted to other women in the past and managed to hang on to his heart. It probably wasn't actually desire he'd felt so briefly...more like compassion and empathy. Yes, that was it. He felt sorry for her. She was so alone, without even the comfort of memories to ease that loneliness. He was responding to her as he would have to anyone in the same predicament. He'd always been drawn to the helpless, it was no wonder he empathized with Jane's dilemma.

Besides, his life was full enough without any personal relationships. He didn't have space for a woman in it. His patients demanded most of his time and energy, leaving very little for anything or anyone else.

Furthermore, of all the women in the world, Jane Smith was definitely one he knew he had to steer clear of. She had a life someplace, and sooner or later she would remember it and return to it. Getting involved with her would be consciously setting himself up for heartbreak. His heart had been broken once and couldn't stand the pain of breaking another time.

When he wheeled into the hospital parking lot, he felt stronger, less tense about his decision to allow Jane to stay with him. He was a grown man, in charge of his own emotions. He would just consider her one of his patients, a woman who required a certain amount of caring and compassion, but who couldn't penetrate any deeper than the surface of his heart. He would never again allow anyone into the core.

Jane wandered the confines of the house, trying to fill the silence of her surroundings, the emptiness of her mind. She still tasted the humiliation she'd felt earlier as she'd been questioned and probed by the people at Social Services. They'd asked her the same questions over and over again, changing them around, disguising them in an attempt to trick her, expose her as an amnesia fake.

A small smile touched her lips as she thought of Frank's defensive anger. He'd demanded to see supervisors in every department they'd gone to, voicing strongly his disapproval at their suggestion that she go to the women's shelter in Wilmington. He'd been Sir Galahad in a doctor's white coat, Lancelot in a sports car.

Her smile faltered slightly as she sank onto the sofa. Frank Longford was not a knight in shining armor. He couldn't ride in on a white horse and rescue her. He was simply a nice doctor who'd found himself embroiled in her life due to circumstances beyond his control.

She was grateful that he was allowing her to stay here, work for him, but he didn't have the power to rescue her from the blackness of her mind. Somehow she knew only she had that power.

She smiled again as Mutt nudged her leg with the tip of his cold, wet nose, obviously seeking some attention. She leaned over and scrubbed him behind his ears, unsurprised when Jeff joined them, impatiently waiting his turn for an ear-scratching.

"So, what do I do now, boys?" she asked as she rose from the sofa and paced the room restlessly. "I've been hired to clean, so I guess that's what I'll do."

She found furniture polish, glass cleaner and scouring powder under the kitchen sink. Thus armed, she spent the next couple of hours cleaning the living room and kitchen.

As she worked, she discovered tidbits of information that painted a more complete picture of the man who owned the house. The bookshelves in the living room were full of mystery novels and the records next to the stereo were mostly instrumentals.

In the kitchen, she found the refrigerator well stocked, and pulled two steaks out of the freezer to thaw. They hadn't specified the extent of her tasks as housekeeper, but surely he wouldn't mind if she had dinner ready for him when he got home from the hospital. She would make a big salad, a couple baked potatoes, then when he got home, she could throw the steaks on the barbecue grill that stood on the deck.

Finished in the kitchen and living room, she moved into the room where she'd slept. There she'd dusted the furniture and cleaned the mirror on the dresser.

After cleaning the bathroom, she hesitated in the doorway of his bedroom, unsure if he would appreciate her efforts or if he would think she'd intruded on his privacy. His room was twice the size of hers. The bed was covered with a geometric-patterned black-and-white spread that matched the curtains.

Where the living room had looked homey and comfortable, this room looked like a place where he spent little time. Pocket change scattered the top of the dresser, along with several bottles of cologne, but that was the only evidence of habitation.

Making her decision, she quickly straightened the covers on the bed, then polished the furniture, surprised at how little personality the room contained.

When she was finished, she closed the door behind her, more intrigued than ever with Frank Longford. He was an attractive man. Why wasn't he married?

Why didn't his bedroom contain any sort of evidence of romantic nights spent with a special woman? He'd told her he'd almost married once. What had happened?

She shoved her questions aside, realizing that perhaps because of her own lack of a past, she was in danger of becoming obsessed with Frank's.

It was nearly five o'clock when she began wondering what time Frank would return home. The salad was made, the potatoes scrubbed and poked and ready to zap in the microwave. The steaks were thawed and ready for the gas grill. She'd reshowered and was dressed in another of the few shorts outfits that comprised her wardrobe. She stood at the door, watching the road outside.

He hadn't said what time he would be back and she had no idea what kind of hours he kept at the hospital. The silence of the house pressed in around her, making her feel an ache of loneliness, a feeling of disconnection with the rest of the world.

In an attempt to alleviate the silence, she placed a stack of records on the stereo, enjoying the sound of music that replaced the empty quiet.

By seven-thirty the sun had sunk low, riding the horizon like a magical flaming orange orb. The dogs stood at the sliding door, whining their need for their nightly run. She remembered they hadn't been out all day, and slid the door open to let them out.

She stepped out onto the deck, the wood, retaining the day's heat, warm beneath her bare feet. She watched the mutts romp in the sand and again wondered where she belonged.

Leaning against the railing, she stared out at the water, watching as the sinking sun bled its crimson onto the waves. Fire. The ocean had become a sea of flames, the descending darkness a wall of smoke.

The beach melted away before her eyes, transformed into a nightmare of smoke and fire...and death. Death surrounded her, embraced her in its icy grip as the vision grew and expanded.

A baby's cry filled her head, a terrified infant's screams. She slapped her hands over her ears to block out the sound, needing to stifle the cries that whirled around and around in her head. She didn't want to hear it. The noise replaced the emptiness inside her with horror so intense, guilt so overwhelming, she cried out and stumbled backward, banging into the sliding glass door.

The abrupt physical jolt made the vision disappear, as if waved away by a magician's wand. The beach stretched before her, not in flames, not smoke-shrouded, but with the falling shadows of night upon it. The cool evening air didn't contain the scent of death, but rather the sharp odor of salt and kelp.

She breathed deeply of the air, clinging to the sound of the wind chimes in the distance, the roar of the waves as they rushed to the shore. No baby's cry. Although it had all been frighteningly vivid, it had all been in her mind.

"Mutt...Jeff," she called, her voice reedy with shock, but they apparently heard her and came bounding back to the house.

She fed them the same dry dog food she'd seen Frank give them the night before, and tried to keep her mind blessedly blank, her emotions firmly in check.

It wasn't until she lay down on the sofa that the shivering swept over her. The shuddering began in her feet, then quickly suffused her entire body as she thought of the vision she'd had on the deck. What did it mean? What *could* it mean?

She curled up, trying to still the convulsive shaking. She hadn't been asleep. She couldn't dismiss the vision as a nightmare...not the way she had dismissed those she'd suffered the night before. She'd been wide-awake out on the deck. She had to face reality. The sight she'd seen in her mind's eye was not a nightmare. It had been a memory...but a memory of what?

Frank smelled her before he saw her. The moment he stepped into the house, his nose picked up the distinctive scents of pine cleaner, furniture polish and whitening cleanser. Immediately following that initial assault, he smelled the faint, floral scent of her perfume. He steeled himself against its evocative whisper, not wanting to think of things feminine and soft.

He looked at his wristwatch and sighed. Nearly midnight. Jane was probably already in bed. He was almost grateful for that. It had been a hellish afternoon and exhaustion tugged heavily on him. He didn't want to have to sort out why all afternoon as he'd worked, he'd been haunted by visions of a pair of green eyes and a wealth of dark, rich hair that made his fingers itch in anticipation of touching its softness.

Anxiety suddenly rose inside him as he realized the dogs hadn't greeted him at the door as was their normal habit. He hurried from the entry hallway into the living room, pausing at the door and drinking in the sight that greeted him.

Jane was asleep on the sofa, the darkness of her hair splayed erotically against the light sand, coral and green colors of the couch. One dog lay on her feet, his head resting on her thigh, the other one was on the floor, his head beneath her motionless hand.

Both dogs acknowledged his presence by wagging their tails, but neither moved from their position of comfort. Traitors, he thought, eyeing them in mock disgust.

Yet, he had to admit that if he had a choice between running to the front door to greet a tired man or remaining curled in comfort next to Jane's sweet scent and warm body, he would definitely choose the latter. This particular thought made a sweeping irritation race through him. An irritation that grew as his gaze swept down the length of her shorts-clad legs. It should be against the law to have legs that long, he thought, tamping down the swift desire that raced through his veins.

"Mutt. Get down," he whispered in command, taking out his sudden vexation on the furry creature who usually wasn't allowed on the sofa. The offender glared at him balefully, then reluctantly yawned and scratched at the area behind one ear. "Mutt," Frank warned. The dog hesitated a moment longer, then jumped down to the floor.

Apparently, the sudden removal of weight on her feet awakened Jane. Her eyelids fluttered open, green orbs soft with slumber. She sat up and shoved her dark mass of hair away from her face. "Oh, you're home." Her voice was heavy with sleep, like a tulip working up to escape the burden of rich soil. "What time is it?"

"Late," he answered tersely.

"I made supper. It will just take a minute to broil the steaks."

He shook his head, half-crazed by the sweeping emotions that stirred within him. "I'm not hungry. I'm going to bed."

He didn't wait to see her reaction to his abruptness. He only knew he needed to escape her, escape the intimacy of the scene around him. The table set for two...a woman awaiting his return...it spoke of dreams he'd long ago abandoned, whispered of emotions he'd long ago decided to deny himself. He didn't want it. He didn't want any of it.

He retreated to his bedroom, but her presence was there, as well. As he deposited his pocket change on top of the dresser and yanked off his tie, he was aware of the lemon scent of furniture polish and the subtle teasing odor of her perfume. Damn...what did the woman do, bathe in the stirring scent?

He walked over to the window, cracking it open to allow in the sea breeze. The tangy air was refreshing, but not cool enough to douse the flames that had ignited in the pit of his stomach.

He'd forgotten what it was like to anticipate returning home after a long day at work. He'd forgotten the pleasure of walking in and knowing somebody had kept a light burning just for him, a meal warm just for him. More than anything, he'd forgotten the evocative excitement of desire... the anticipation of experiencing intimacy with a special woman.

But for just a moment, Jane had made him remember all of it... all the wonderful, intimate, passionate things he'd once wanted for himself.

"Damn her," he muttered as he pulled off the remainder of his clothes and crawled beneath the crisp, clean sheets. He'd been comfortable with his particular form of selective amnesia.

He closed his eyes, trying to shut out his mental visions of the way she had looked when he'd walked into the house. Her dark hair fanned out, her mouth parted slightly as if in unconscious invitation, those tantalizing legs that seemed to extend forever below the skimpy shorts... He groaned out loud and squeezed his eyes more tightly closed in his efforts to suppress the erotic images that danced in his head. Whatever happened to sugarplums? he wondered humorlessly.

He had a feeling that in offering Jane the position as his housekeeper, by inviting her into his home, he had managed to make the biggest mistake of his life.

Chapter 5

Jane stumbled from the bed, grabbed one of the shorts outfits from the dresser drawer, then headed for the bathroom. A sleepy smile crossed her face as she thought of the pleasure of standing beneath an early-morning shower. She reached out for the knob of the bathroom door, gasping in surprise as Frank walked out . . . and right into her.

His hands grasped her shoulders in an attempt to keep them both from tumbling over, and in that instant she was surrounded by the pleasant scent of tangy mint soap and spicy after-shave.

Beneath her fingertips, his chest was still damp and contained a heat that made her want to curl up against it. She could feel the warmth of his fingers burning through the thin material of her cotton nightgown.

She didn't remember her identity, didn't know where she had been or where she belonged. But her mind instantly knew the emotion that whirled through her as she remained against the strength and warmth of his body.

He released her as if she were a flaming torch, and grabbed for the towel that was tucked carelessly around his waist. "Sorry," she murmured as she awkwardly stepped farther away from him. "I didn't know you were in there."

"No problem," he replied, moving past her and disappearing into his bedroom while Jane escaped into the bathroom.

The remaining steam from his hot shower swirled around her as she adjusted the water temperature. It surrounded her in its damp warmth, reminding her of the feel of his skin beneath her fingertips.

She undressed and stepped in beneath the warm spray. Tilting her head forward, she allowed the water to cascade down her back, trying to forget that moment in the hallway, the moment of intimacy that had shaken her so.

It amazed her that her mind refused to let her know her favorite color, the secrets of her past, but had immediately recognized and identified desire. The last thing she needed to do was get tangled up in a relationship with Frank when she didn't even have a relationship with herself.

She sighed at this thought. She'd gotten no more flashes of vision, no more pieces of memory throughout the night. Although she supposed she should be grateful that she hadn't suffered any nightmares; her sleep had been deep and dreamless.

She shut off the shower and got out, reaching for a towel from the stack in the linen closet. As she dried herself and dressed in the shorts and blouse, she found her thoughts once again drifting to Frank.

She'd been disappointed when he'd gone to bed directly after getting home the night before. As she'd put away the food she'd prepared, she had consoled herself with the fact that he'd worked long hours and must have been exhausted.

Surely the tension she'd felt in the air and his edge of irritation had been a figment of her imagination or a result of his exhaustion. She'd been groggy and he'd been tired and that had colored her perception of his tone of voice and the look on his face.

Still, she couldn't seem to release the idea that he'd been angry... and she wasn't sure why, but his ire seemed to have been directed at her.

She brushed out the wet strands of her hair, then left the bathroom and went into the kitchen to start breakfast. She'd just filled the skillet with strips of bacon, and the coffee had just finished gurgling through the machine, when Frank joined her.

"Don't cook anything for me," he protested, pouring himself a cup of coffee. "I just have time to drink this, then I need to get to my office. I've got some paperwork to take care of before my first patient arrives at eight."

"Surely you should eat something," Jane insisted. "At least a piece of toast."

He shook his head and sipped his coffee, his gaze not meeting hers. Jane frowned, once again aware of a sudden tension in the air, a tension that was distinctly uncomfortable.

"Frank," she began hesitantly, "is something wrong? I mean, maybe this whole arrangement isn't such a good idea."

"No, nothing is wrong and the arrangement is fine." Still he didn't meet her gaze. "I've just got a lot on my mind."

"Are you sure?" she pressed. No matter what her own personal circumstances, she didn't want to stay where she wasn't wanted. She had a feeling she'd never depended much on anyone in whatever life she'd previously had.

"I'm sure." His eyes finally met hers, dark and enigmatic, they told her nothing of what he felt. As she watched, the irises darkened further and a frown puckered his forehead. "Don't you have anything to wear other than shorts?"

She looked at him in confusion, and self-consciously touched the material at the hips of the cotton shorts. Why on earth would he care what she wore? "Actually, I don't. The suitcase the police brought to me didn't exactly contain an array of choices. Four pairs of shorts, three blouses and an unimaginative selection of sturdy cotton undies." She stared at him, amazed to see faint spots of color appear on either cheek.

"When I get back this evening, we'll go downtown and pick up a few more things for you."

"I can't let you do that," she protested. "You've done more than enough for me already."

"We'll consider it an advance on your first week's salary."

"But that's really not necessary."

His eyes flickered down the length of her, then narrowed. He finished the last of his coffee, slamming his cup down on the table with more force than necessary. "Yes, it *is* necessary." Without waiting for her reply, he disappeared into the hallway and out the front door.

Jane stared after him for a long moment, then turned and eyed the dogs lying beneath the kitchen table. "Well, somebody definitely got up on the wrong side of the bed," she exclaimed.

As she worked to clean up the breakfast she had started to make, she wondered what kind of life she'd had before. Had she worked? What sort of skills did she have? Was she a professional? A waitress? Nothing she could think of felt right. Nothing caused a light of recognition to even faintly burn in her brain.

At least the police had her name and were working to find the pertinent facts to her life. If somebody could just tell her one single fact about herself, she felt that the memories would come tumbling back. It was like a dam holding back the force of massive water. All she needed was a tiny crack for it all to give way.

Minutes later, she let the dogs outside and joined them in their early-morning romp on the beach. It didn't take long for her to tire. She sank onto the sand and watched as the dogs chased each other in circles, snapping at the morning breeze and nosing pieces of kelp and shells that had washed up overnight.

She sighed and tilted her head up toward the warmth of the sun. If only somebody could tell her the little things about herself that gave her a real identity. Did she have a temper? Was she selfish? What did she do in her spare time? Had she ever been in love? Without those particular pieces, she was just a name...a body without a soul, a person without a place. Where did she belong?

She closed her eyes, a picture of Frank immediately filling her mind. With the towel draped carelessly around his slender hips, and his dark hair tousled and damp from the shower, she'd immediately wanted to grab him by the hand and lead him into his bedroom. She'd wanted him to abolish the darkness in her head with the mindless pleasure of passion.

Had she somehow communicated to him that momentary lapse of good sense? Was that what had made him so abrupt, so eager to escape to his office?

She knew she'd be a fool to make love with Frank. Even not knowing anything else about herself, she knew it would be the stupidest thing she could ever do.

She was in no position to become involved with anyone. The ache inside her had nothing to do with the need to connect with a man; it had everything to do with the need to discover herself. She would be a complete fool to confuse the two.

Still, she couldn't ignore that there was a certain chemistry between Frank and herself, an attraction that had appeared the moment they had left the hospital. She also knew she wasn't the only one who felt it. It had flamed in his eyes for a brief instant when she'd bumped into him in the hallway that morning.

However, it was equally obvious to her that he had no more of a wish to follow through on it than she did. He was a solitary man, and she was a woman without a past.

With a sigh, she stood up and brushed the sand off her bottom. "Mutt . . . Jeff . . ." She smiled as the two dogs bounded back, their tongues lolling out as they panted from their exertions.

Throughout the day, as she cleaned, she kept the stereo on, needing to fill up the emptiness not only of the house, but her head. She discovered she liked Frank's collection of music, found the soft instrumentals soothing to the edge of anxiety that never quite dissipated and instead swirled inside her with a litany of unanswered questions.

At noon, the phone rang. It was Frank's receptionist telling Jane to expect him home by five o'clock. She thanked the woman and hung up, knowing that Frank had called so she'd be ready to leave for the shopping trip into town the minute he walked in the door.

By five o'clock, she was ready for his return. Although he hadn't mentioned anything about the evening meal, Jane had prepared it and had it ready to serve the moment he walked in. Surely he wanted to eat before they embarked on their shopping trip.

The dogs heard his approach before she did. They ran to the door and studied the wooden barrier expectantly. A moment later, it opened and he walked in, bringing the life back into the house.

Jane could tell immediately that he was in a better mood than he'd been in the night before. As he greeted the dogs, patting them affectionately on the head, the lines of his face were relaxed into a smile that radiated a magic warmth, a warmth Jane instantly wanted to step into, be surrounded by.

"Hi," she said. "Good day?"

He nodded, giving the dogs a final pat. "All ready to go?" he asked.

"I thought you might want to eat first." He hesitated and she hurriedly added, "It's all ready."

"Okay," he agreed, following her into the kitchen.

"It's the strangest thing," Jane began, anxious to fill the silence that stretched for a moment between them as he took a seat at the table. "I don't remember anything about myself. My name doesn't even feel like my own, yet I didn't have to use a recipe for the chicken casserole I made. I just knew it."

"Amnesia is one of the oddest things doctors ever see," he answered. He leaned back in the chair, obviously at ease with the topic of conversation. "There's often no rhyme or reason for the tidbits of information the brain retains with amnesia. It's one of the most perplexing things to try to understand."

"I don't want to understand it, I just want it to go away," Jane exclaimed, setting the salad and the casserole on the table, then sitting down across from him. "Now, tell me all about your day."

He looked at her in surprise and again she realized he wasn't a man accustomed to sharing the pieces of his life with anyone. "It was pretty much a usual day at the office."

Jane smiled at him. "Could you please elaborate a little more on that? I'm not a doctor, so I don't know what a usual day is like."

He returned her smile. "The day began with a standing appointment I have with an eighty-three-year-old woman. She comes in to see me every Tuesday and Thursday morning at eight o'clock."

"Those are a lot of office visits. What's the matter with her?"

"Not a thing. She's the healthiest woman I've ever seen."

Jane frowned. "Then why the semiweekly visits?"

"Loneliness. She never married, and lived with her sister all her life. The sister died a year ago, and since then, she's developed all kinds of maladies to bring her in to see me. But the only thing she really needs is somebody to spend some time with her, talk with her."

"How sad," Jane murmured, thinking of the kind of loneliness that would drive an old woman to seek comfort from a visit with the doctor.

"On a lighter note, my next patient was my patient from hell." Jane laughed. "She's a six-year-old who hates physicals, hates injections and especially hates me." Frank grinned, enjoying the sound of her laughter. She was a woman meant to laugh often, and from that moment on, he regaled her with story after story, his goal to keep the laughter sparkling in her eyes and curving her lips.

The stories continued as they finished the meal and took off toward town. The evening air was warm and fragrant with the scent of summer.

"Too much wind?" Frank asked, noting the way her hair whipped around her face, wrapped lovingly around her neck.

"No. It's wonderful," she assured him. "I love summer."

He looked at her sideways. "Is that a memory?"

Her forehead wrinkled. "I'm not sure. It might be...or it might just be a decisive opinion I formed at this very moment."

He laughed. "Then I agree with your decisive opinion. Summer is my favorite time of year, too." He frowned as they drove past a row of shops. "I'm really not sure of the best place to get women's clothes. I've got a patient who runs a boutique and I thought that might be the best place."

"Anywhere is fine. All I really need is one or two pairs of slacks."

Frank cast a surreptitious gaze at the glorious length of her legs.... He'd be grateful when she had a pair of pants covering their smooth silkiness. In the last twenty-four hours, he'd developed something of a fixation, wondering if her skin was really as smooth as it looked, speculating on how her long legs would feel wrapped firmly around his.

He sighed with relief as he saw the shop he'd been looking for. He parked the car directly in front, and they went inside the bright interior of Sarah's Styles.

"Hi, Dr. Longford," Sarah Burnside greeted him, her gaze immediately going to Jane with interest. "What brings you into my humble shop?"

"Uh...we need to pick up some things for Jane." He quickly introduced the two women. "She needs some slacks, and maybe a dress and a bathing suit." Frank was aware of Sarah's speculative grin, the quizzical tilt of her eyebrows and it merely increased his discomfort. "Anyway, just get her whatever she needs and send the bill to my office." He turned to Jane. "I'll just wait across the street in the café."

The moment he left the shop, Sarah turned to Jane, her blue eyes sparkling with friendliness. "You a relative of the doctor's?"

"No...I work for him," Jane answered, wishing Frank hadn't left her alone to field the barrage of questions she expected to follow. "I'm his...uh... housekeeper. It's just a temporary thing...until I locate some of my family...." Jane knew she was babbling, saying far more than necessary.

"Say, are you the one he found on the beach? The amnesia woman?" Sarah's eyes widened and her auburn curls danced around her face as if in anticipation. Jane hesitated a moment, then nodded, surprised when Sarah immediately placed an arm around her shoulders. "You poor dear. It must be frightening, not to know anything about yourself."

"Frightening and more than a little bit frustrating," Jane admitted, touched by the woman's obvious show of support. "I don't even know what size I wear," she said, hoping to sway the woman's attention back to the business at hand.

Sarah stepped back from Jane and studied her critically. "Probably a five or a six."

Although the size fives fit perfectly in the waist and hips, the length was a bit short, requiring her to go to the sixes. Jane found two pairs of slacks, one black and one white, figuring the two basic colors would go with any of the blouses she had.

"Dr. Longford also mentioned you needed a dress and a bathing suit," Sarah reminded Jane, leading her over to a rack of swimwear.

"Oh, I really don't think a swimsuit is necessary," Jane protested. She didn't want to take advantage of Frank's generosity.

"Of course it's necessary," Sarah countered. "It's June and you're in Garett Beach. Everyone owns at least one bathing suit." She pulled a hot-pink bikini from the rack and held it out toward Jane. "You'd look terrific in this."

"Oh, no...I don't think so...not a bikini." Jane blanched at the thought of the skimpy suit. "I think a one-piece is much more my style."

Sarah sighed regretfully. "Why is it women who can wear bikinis don't, and the ones who shouldn't always do?" She pulled several one-pieces off the rack and handed them to Jane. "You'd better go try these on, they don't always run true to size."

As Jane tried on the suits, Sarah kept up a steady stream of chatter about the town, her husband, Tom, and finally Frank. "There was a time when he was considered the catch of the town. Everybody who had a daughter, sister or friend the right age paraded them into his office hoping that Cupid would make a love connection. But since the fiasco with Gloria, he's closed himself off from people. He's the greatest with doctor/patient relationships, but he keeps a distance the rest of the time."

"I'll take the blue one," Jane said as she stepped out of the dressing room and handed Sarah the suits. "Who was Gloria?"

"A tourist. She came to town, all blond and vivacious, and she and Dr. Longford hit it off. Talk around town was that the most eligible bachelor had finally been bitten by the love bug. Rumor had it they were planning a wedding. I don't know what happened, but one day she up and left town and nobody ever saw her again. The doctor was never quite the same after that. I think when Gloria left town, she took his heart and soul with her." Sarah shook her head sadly, then grinned slyly. "Of course, with your being with him every day and night, maybe you can help him find his heart again."

Jane shook her head and smiled self-consciously. "I'm just there temporarily. Besides, I've got quite a chunk of myself missing. I think perhaps I'd better work on finding that."

It only took them another couple of minutes to find a mint-green cotton sundress to add to the purchases;

then, packages in hand, Jane went across the street to the café to find Frank.

He sat in a booth by himself, a piece of pie and a cup of coffee before him. He smiled as she slid into the booth across from him. "Want a piece of pie? I can personally vouch for the cherry and the apple."

She laughed. "You had both?"

He nodded. "Guilty. I'm a sucker for pie. I think in another lifetime I must have been Mrs. Smith's son."

Jane's smile faltered slightly. "I don't care about discovering who I was in a past lifetime. It would be nice to know what's going on in this one." She wanted to ask him about Gloria, but knew instinctively he would resent the fact that Sarah had shared private pieces of his life with her. "I would love a cup of coffee," she said, instead.

"Did Sarah take good care of you?" he asked once the waitress had brought her coffee.

"Yes, she seems very nice."

"She is nice. Her husband is the mayor of Garett Beach and Sarah is one of his best assets. She has a heart of gold." He looked at her knowingly. "And I'll bet she managed to get all kinds of information out of you." He laughed at Jane's expression. "Yes, that's another of Sarah's endearing characteristics. She makes it her business to know everyone else's business."

"Then I suppose by tomorrow, everyone in town will know that you have a housekeeper who has amnesia," Jane observed, noting how the artificial lights of the café drew out brilliant sparks of fire in his dark hair.

His grin widened. "Oh, well, it won't be the first time I've been the talk of the town." He stood up. "Ready? I'd sort of like to get back and have a run on the beach with the mutts before it gets too dark."

She nodded and quickly finished her coffee. As he paid the cashier, Jane found herself studying him, enjoying the way the lines of his face creased upward, as if his face was accustomed to smiles rather than frowns.

She was grateful that at the moment, the smile lines were deep, without the tension that had tugged them downward the night before. She was also grateful that the inexplicable tension that had existed between them that morning was gone, leaving only a familiarity that was strangely comforting.

The ride home was pleasant, filled with small talk that encouraged the mood to continue. When they got back to the house, Frank disappeared into his bedroom to change into jogging clothes, and Jane changed into a pair of her new slacks.

She heard Frank and the dogs leave by the back door and she moved outside to the deck and sat down. The sun was setting, casting twilight gold all around, painting the man and the dogs on the beach in shimmering tones. She saw the bronzed muscles of Frank's calves bunching with his exertions, noted his fine physical condition as he raced the dogs down the sandy shore.

She turned her gaze in the other direction, where even the lush light of dusk couldn't camouflage the unsightly buildings with their aura of hopelessness. What was I doing there? she wondered, a ball of despair forming in the center of her chest. It was obviously a place for the down-and-out, the victims and losers of life. It was a home for the forgotten, the hiding, the hunted.

And which one am I? The question pounded in her head, creating an ache in the center of her forehead. She rubbed at it with two fingers. What if she never remembered? What if the amnesia never went away? It was a horrifying thought, one she refused to entertain for more than a single minute.

She quickly returned her attention to Frank, who approached much more slowly than when he'd jogged off. She grinned, seeing his broad chest rapidly rising and falling from his run. "I think the dogs won," she said in amusement, pointing to where the dogs still frolicked with the boundless energy and enthusiasm of children.

"Whew, I think you're right." He flopped down on one of the colorful deck chairs. "I've really allowed myself to get out of shape."

Jane said nothing, although she thought she'd never seen a man who looked more in shape. The jogging shorts exposed most of the muscular legs covered with springy dark hairs, and emphasized the firm tautness of his buttocks. The T-shirt stretched tightly across his broad shoulders and chest, and displayed the lean flatness of his abdomen. Out of shape? Not in this lifetime.

"Uh...would you like a glass of iced tea?" she asked, fighting against the inner rise of heat that made her feel as if she'd swallowed a chunk of the sun.

"That sounds great," he agreed.

She escaped into the kitchen and poured them each a tall glass of tea. She paused a moment to rub an ice cube across her forehead, hoping it would alleviate the heat that suffused her.

What's the matter with me? she wondered irritably. It didn't seem fair she should suffer not only a severe case of amnesia but a case of raging hormones, as well. She threw the half-melted ice cube she'd been rubbing on her forehead into the sink and grabbed the two glasses of tea.

"Here you go," she said as she returned to the deck.

His fingers lightly brushed against hers as he took the glass from her. A surge of renewed heat shot up her arm and into the pit of her stomach.

She sat down on one of the other chairs, wondering if sudden bursts of heat were a common side effect of amnesia. She sipped the sweet cold tea and looked out to where the sun was sending its last gasp of color onto the horizon.

You're just confused, she assured herself. You're feeling displaced and more than a little bit afraid. At the moment, Frank seems the only sane and dependable thing in your life. It's no wonder your emotions are all jumbled up where he's concerned.

"I spoke to a colleague about you today," Frank said, pulling her from her reverie.

"A colleague?" She looked at him curiously.

"Dr. Wilton. Harry Wilton. He's a psychologist. He'd like to see you . . . see if he can help you remember."

"Yes. Yes, I'd like that," she said decisively. "I need to do something. The memories aren't exactly flooding back with any regularity."

Frank nodded. "I'll call him tomorrow and see what can be set up." He finished drinking his tea and stood up. "I think I'll move inside for a shower." He whistled for the dogs, who came running.

"I'll just stay out here a little longer," she replied.

As he and the dogs disappeared into the house, Jane once again gazed into the distance. The sound of the waves coupled with the gentle tinkle of the wind chimes and for a moment Jane knew complete peace.

She didn't know how long she sat there, not thinking but rather just experiencing the beauty surrounding her. It wasn't until Frank opened the door that she realized she must have been there for quite some time as the night had taken over and the darkness was as profound as that which shrouded her mind.

"Jane? There's somebody here to see you. It's one of the policemen who's been working on your case."

She followed Frank inside, her heart pounding with rapid intensity. Maybe the police have discovered something, she thought hopefully. Maybe he's here to tell me where I live, where I belong.

The policeman sat on the sofa, eyed dubiously by a dog on either side of him. He stood as Jane and Frank entered the room, looking relieved as the dogs moved away from him. "Hi, I'm Officer Martin."

Jane shook his hand, then sat down in the chair across from him. She recognized him as one of the officers who'd brought her belongings to the hospital. She leaned forward eagerly. "You've found out something?"

The officer hesitated, worrying the rim of his hat between two fingers. Jane was aware of Frank moving to stand next to her chair, as if sensing the officer was not there to deliver good news. "We ran your name and approximate age through the computers. We checked DMV and social security..."

"And?" Jane held her breath.

"And we can't find you."

She frowned. "What do you mean you can't find me?"

"I mean there's no record of a Jane Smith your age and physical description existing anywhere."

"I'm afraid I don't understand." Confusion swirled in her mind and she was vaguely conscious of Frank placing a firm hand on her shoulder.

The officer shrugged, looking uncomfortable. "The only thing we can figure is that the name you used to check in to that beachfront cabin was an alias."

"An alias?" She looked at him incredulously. "You mean Jane Smith isn't really my name?"

The officer offered her a crooked grin. "Not unless you grew in a poppy patch without any form of documentation or identification." He stood up.

"Am I in trouble...legally, or something?" she asked vaguely.

"For checking into a motel under a false name?" He shook his head and emitted a small chuckle. "If that were the case, we'd have to build a million more jails just to hold all the cheating husbands and wives of the world." His smile faltered and he shifted from foot to foot. "Well, we just felt you needed to know this as soon as possible."

"Thank you, Officer Martin," Frank said.

Jane watched dully as Frank walked the officer to the front door. She stood up and moved to the window, staring out into the blackness of the night. She was numb. What little sanity she'd maintained up until this moment now threatened to desert her like a rat jumping off a sinking ship.

"Jane...are you all right?" Frank asked softly.

She felt his presence directly behind her. She smelled the pleasant scent, minty soap and after-shave, the remnants of his recent shower. As he placed his hands on her shoulders, she sank back against the warmth of his body. She wanted to melt into him, dwell forever in the strength and support she felt emanating from him.

"No," she whispered hoarsely. "No, I'm not all right, and I'm so afraid I'll never be all right ever again."

He turned her around to face him and drew her into a strong embrace. She twined her arms around his neck, allowing him to be her rock as her world turned topsy-turvy. As the complete realization of what the officer had told her sank in, she clung more tightly to Frank, her eyes misting with tears of frustration and fear.

"Shh," he crooned softly, stroking her hair as his arms provided her a momentary shelter from the storm. "It will be all right. I promise it will all be okay. You're going to be just fine."

But she didn't feel as if she was going to be fine. She was scared and her fear caused her body to tremble uncontrollably against his.

If what the officer had said was true, then why had she been using a false name? Who was she? Question after question whirled around and around in her head, causing her to feel both dizzy and slightly nauseous at the same time.

"It's bad enough that I don't know anything at all about myself. But at least before now, I had a name, a place to begin. Now I don't even have that. I've got nothing... nothing." She shuddered and drew a deep breath, trying to still her tears.

Frank led her over to the sofa, keeping her in the haven of his arms. They sat down, and with a finger he swiped her cheeks, removing the tears that lingered there. "Okay, so we now know what name definitely is not yours... that's a beginning," he offered.

She stared at him wordlessly. The sob that she had been about to release turned into a giggle as she registered the total ridiculousness of what he'd said.

"That's better," he said gently. "Your face was meant for smiles, not tears." The smile on his face slowly faded and Jane watched as the brown of his eyes deepened in hue, warmed her with their intensity.

She suddenly knew he was going to kiss her. She also recognized it would be a big mistake, something they would both probably deeply regret.

But even knowing this, she parted her lips, eagerly accepting his mouth as it descended on hers.

Chapter 6

Frank hadn't intended to kiss her. And the moment his lips touched hers, he knew he was in deep trouble. Her mouth was achingly soft and warm, moist and sweet. She opened up beneath him, blossoming like a rose to the warmth of the sun. He drank deeply of her, feeling more than a little bit intoxicated by her heat, her scent and her honeyed taste.

He could feel the press of her rounded breasts against his chest and felt the immediate response of his own body. Swift and mighty, his desire was immediate, surging through him like a tingling electrical current. The intensity shocked him, frightened him, and he instantly broke the kiss and moved away from her.

"I'm sorry," he said, rising from the sofa in the

need to distance himself from her. "That shouldn't have happened. Please forget it did."

Her eyes were a deep bottle green, still heavy with the trace of tears. "No problem," she said hesitantly, her voice slightly deeper than usual. She looked at him searchingly for a long moment. "Forgetting is the one thing I do best."

As he saw her halfhearted smile, he fought the impulse to gather her back into his arms. He admired her courage, the sense of humor that never quite deserted her. Despite her amnesia, he again sensed an enormous strength inside her, a strength that would carry her through this mess.

"I think I'll go on to bed," she said as she rose from the sofa.

She was almost to the door when he called her name. She turned back and looked at him. "It really will be all right," he said softly.

She nodded, then without a backward glance, she went into the bedroom and closed the door behind her.

Frank watched her go, fighting the need to follow, shoulder the fear he knew must underlie the strength, the apprehension beneath the jaunty humor.

She has a life, he reminded himself, and he had to keep his distance.

He went into the bathroom and brushed his teeth, hoping the wintergreen gel toothpaste would remove the taste of her from his mouth. It didn't. As he fell asleep, his head was filled with the memory of their kiss.

* * *

"Hey, Frank."

Frank turned to see Russ Waylon walking down the hospital corridor toward him. "Hi, Russ, what's up?"

"That's just what I was going to ask you, you old dog." Russ elbowed him in the ribs and grinned slyly. "What's this I hear about your having a new house-keeper?"

"Ah, I wondered how long it would be before the talented gossips of Garett Beach would be flapping their jaws," Frank returned dryly.

"So it's true?" Russ's eyebrows danced up and down in a Groucho Marx imitation. "You old fox, you," he said with a chuckle.

"It's true, but you can wipe that ridiculous expression off your face and stop chortling. It's all completely innocent."

Russ sighed in disappointment. "Yeah, that's just what I was afraid of." He eyed Frank wryly. "There are times I worry about you, my friend."

"Worry?"

"I'd worry about any single man that has a woman who looks like Jane Smith living in his house and keeps things completely innocent."

"You know me, the happy solitary man. She just needed some help. Social Services was going to put her up in the shelter in Wilmington and I couldn't stand the thought of that. You knew I'd been talking about hiring somebody to take care of the house. It just seemed a reasonable option to have her work for me while she works on getting her memory back."

"Any progress in that area?" Russ asked curiously, his expression once again that of a professional.

"Not much. I've put in a call to Harry Wilton. At the moment, he's on vacation, but I'm hoping as soon as he gets back into town, he'll take her on as a patient and see if he can help her."

"Sounds like a wise idea," Russ agreed. "Harry is a good man."

"I hope so. She's more of a mystery now than she was when I brought her into the hospital." Frank hesitated a moment, then continued, "The police came by the other night and told us the name she'd used to check into that beachfront cabin wasn't hers. Apparently, she was using an alias."

Russ released a low whistle. "That doesn't sound too good. Perhaps you're wise to keep things innocent." He looked at his wristwatch and frowned. "Oh, gotta run. Hey, this is your weekend off...have a great one." With a smile and a wave, Russ hurried down the corridor.

Frank continued toward the doctors' lounge, where he had been headed before Russ stopped him. He was relieved to find the small room empty.

He poured himself a cup of the inklike coffee and sat down at the mock-wood table. Sipping from the mug, he leaned back in the chair and replayed in his mind the conversation with Russ.

It had been three days since he'd tasted Jane's lips, and since that time, everything had remained completely innocent between them...everything but his thoughts. And his thoughts were distinctly erotic where Jane was concerned.

Thankfully, his work hours were long so it was late when he got home each evening, effectively cutting into the time he spent with her. However, he found himself caught in a curious dichotomy of emotions. He enjoyed her company, loved to hear her laughter as he shared the lighter moments of his day with her. He was half-crazed by her subtle sensuality, the sweet floral scent of her hair, the graceful movements of those long legs. Yes, he liked to be with her...and he dreaded each moment spent in her company.

It worried him that she had been using a false name at the cottages. Why would a woman check into a motel using an alias? Had she been running away from someone? Who? He couldn't imagine that she'd done anything wrong, that she was a criminal of some sort. She just wasn't the type. Her eyes were too soft, too full of innocence.

He finished his coffee, stood up and looked at his watch, suddenly anxious to get home. He had two more patients to check on and then his weekend officially began.

He didn't try to analyze why he was looking forward to the weekend when always before he'd lingered at the hospital on Friday nights, in no hurry to get to the emptiness of his home.

Nearly an hour later, he stepped out of the heat of the day and into the air-conditioning of his entryway. "Hello?" he called.

"In here," Jane's voice drifted to him from someplace in the back of the house. As Frank walked down the hallway, he heard the sounds of splashing water and smelled the fragrant scent of bubble bath. The bathroom door was open as if in invitation, but he hesitated just outside, unsure what to expect.

His mind filled with an image of her in a tubful of bubbles, the swell of her breasts visible just above the foaming water. Her legs would be bent at the knees, the shortness of the tub unable to accommodate their length. Her hair would cling to her shoulders, wet silk caressing satin skin. Heat infused him at the vividness of the image. His hands itched and he clenched them into fists, realizing the palms were sweaty.

"Frank? Are you there?" Her words were followed by the sound of splashing water.

He cleared his throat. "Yes . . . yes, I'm here." His voice sounded funny to his ears. Thin and reedy, it squeaked out of him, half-constricted by his mental turmoil.

"Come on in," her voice called out.

He moved forward on legs that suddenly felt like jelly, the fire inside him burning like a raging inferno.

The tub was full of water and bubbles, but it didn't contain Jane. Mutt stood in the water, his expression a mix of humiliation and shame. His fur was covered with foaming soap and Jane crooned softly to him as she poured a pitcher of water over his flanks.

"What are you doing?" Frank asked inanely. The heat inside him cooled with a curious sigh of disappointment and relief.

"I let the two of them out earlier for a little run on the beach and they disappeared. I don't know where they went or what they did, but they both came back covered in muck and mud." She grinned up at him, her smile reigniting the flame in the pit of his stomach. "I've never seen a dog who hates baths as much as this one."

"They rarely get baths," Frank answered, trying not to notice how wet her blouse was...wet enough to turn the pale pink material nearly transparent. "Where's Jeff?" he asked as he consciously tugged his gaze away from her.

"Last time I saw him, he was hiding behind the sofa. He knows he's next."

Frank gazed back at Mutt, his eyes widening as he realized the sudsy dog's intent. "Watch out...he's going to—" Before Frank could complete his warning, Mutt seemed to expand and grow in size, and with a howl of displeasure, he shook. Globs of soap and water flew around the room, decorating Jane's hair and face, slapping across the mirror, even reaching the front of Frank's shirt.

Frank was unable to contain a burst of laughter as he saw the white foam that decorated the tip of her nose and dotted the side of her neck.

"Don't laugh," Jane exclaimed in mock indignation, scrubbing at the bubbles on her nose with the back of one hand. "This dog has no manners at all." Mutt whined as if to protest her words and placed one wet paw on her shoulder. "Oh, no, you don't," she said, removing the paw and pushing Mutt to sit in the water. "As soon as I finish with him, I'll wash Jeff, then I'll get dinner started. I thought I'd cook hamburgers out on the grill."

"Tell you what...while you're wrestling the dogs, I'll cook the burgers," Frank offered.

"That would be terrific," she agreed, smiling at him with the bright expression that once again caused a burst of warmth to flood through him.

Minutes later, as she washed Jeff, Jane's thoughts drifted to Frank. He was home earlier than he'd been in the past three evenings, and she was pleased that he seemed to be in a good humor.

Over the past four days of living with Frank, she had quickly gotten a picture of his work schedule and had come to the conclusion that he carried the load of two doctors. Not only did he have the patients at his own practice and his hospital routine, but he also put in several hours a week at a nearby clinic and was on staff at a nursing home. It was a lot of work for one man, and the long hours showed on him each evening when he finally got home.

She finished up with Jeff, laughing as he ran out of the bathroom as if shot from a cannon. She quickly cleaned up the bathroom, then changed into the cool, mint-green sundress.

She found Frank standing in front of the gas grill on the deck. Clad in brown shorts and a casual pullover shirt, he looked relaxed and handsome.

"Rare or well done?" he asked.

"Definitely well done. Is there anything I can do? Set the table?"

He shook his head, the evening sunlight painting an auburn glow over the dark strands. "Let's paper-plate it and eat out here. There's a nice breeze coming off the water."

"Sounds great to me." She sat down and watched as he flipped and pressed the sizzling patties. He paused a moment and took a long drink from a can of beer. He grinned as he noticed her watching him.

"Ah, there's nothing better than a cold beer after a long day at work. Why don't I grab you one?"

She nodded and he disappeared into the house. He returned a moment later with another can. "You look like the kind of classy woman who'd drink it out of a glass, but you can't really get the full refreshing effect unless you drink it straight." He popped the tab and handed it to her.

She sipped the cold beer and sat back, enjoying the pleasant evening breeze wafting off the water and Frank's company. "This is so nice," she finally said, breaking the comfortable silence between them.

"It is, isn't it? Although it's quite different in the wintertime when the damp air seems to seep into your very bones." He smiled, then returned to the task of removing the cooked patties from the grill. Jane started to rise from the chair, but he stopped her. "Just sit. What do you want on yours? Mustard... ketchup... pickles... ?"

"Everything," she answered. Once again, he went inside and Jane gazed out toward the water, enjoying the tranquility of the scenery, the momentary quiet of her mind. All day long, her head raced with question after question, searching for fragments of memories she could claim as her past. Thankfully, she'd suffered no more of the horrible nightmares and she was beginning to believe that the visions of fire, those dreams of death, had nothing to do with memories at all. In fact, she'd decided that the dreams and images had merely been the reflection of her mental chaos.

"Ah, here we are, a truly American gourmet meal," Frank said as he stepped back out on the deck, a serving tray holding their plates. "We've got overcooked hamburgers, a mound of potato chips and enormous dill pickles."

"Add a cold beer and a gorgeous sunset, and I don't think we're in Kansas anymore, Toto," Jane replied, pulling her chair up to the table. She tilted her head to the side and frowned. "It's the weirdest thing...what the mind remembers."

He smiled sympathetically. "You mean, why is it you can remember a line from the *Wizard of Oz*, but can't remember your own name?"

She nodded, pausing a moment to crunch into a chip. "I went through your record collection this morning and noticed you have a lot of show tunes. I put a couple on and listened to them while I cleaned, and suddenly I realized that I know all the words to Ado Annie's songs."

He eyed her curiously. "I'm sure I should know this, but who on earth is Ado Annie?"

"A character from the musical *Oklahoma*."

"Oh, yes, now I remember." He gestured for her to continue.

"Anyway, I was standing in the middle of the living room singing all the words to one of the songs and it was then that I realized I've played that part in a play. I think it was a high-school production." She picked up another chip, stared at it thoughtfully, then looked back at Frank. "What I don't understand is why the memories that are coming back are so stupid. I'm remembering all the unimportant details of my life, but none of the important ones."

"You're remembering all the safe ones," he said softly.

She looked at him quizzically, noting the liquid depths of his eyes, like pools of dark mocha. They warmed her as effectively as the last lingering rays of sunshine. "What do you mean by safe?"

"If your amnesia is psychologically based as we think it is, then it was probably a trauma that made your mind shut down. For now, the memories that are surfacing are nonthreatening." He reached across the table and took her hand in his. "The rest of it will come back when your mind thinks you're ready."

She nodded, comforted by the assurance in his tone. With a smile, she squeezed his hand, feeling the warmth of the connection race straight to her heart. For a moment, their gazes remained connected, seeking . . . revealing . . .

"I don't know what I'd do without you," she murmured.

"I'm sure you'd be fine," he said, extracting his hand from hers. "I have a feeling you're a survivor,

Jane Smith. Now, we'd better finish eating before our burgers get cold.''

She felt him emotionally distance himself and a strange regret filled her. For that brief moment, when their eyes had touched, their hearts had spoken. It had been the quiet murmur of uncertainty, the heated whisper of suppressed desire.

"Frank, do you think it's possible that the hospital could use me for a few hours a week as a volunteer?" she asked suddenly.

"Why?" he asked in surprise.

She shrugged, toying with the pickle on her plate. "There really isn't much to do around here, and Mutt and Jeff are okay, but they're lousy at conversation. Surely there's something I could do to fill the hours of the day and feel useful."

"Sure, I could talk to Etta and see what we could set up. I never thought about your getting lonely here."

"It's not lonely," she protested. "At least not exactly." Although she did have a deep well of loneliness inside, one she knew came from the fact that she felt so unconnected from everything and everyone. "It just somehow seems wrong to have so many empty hours in a day. It feels unnatural. I know it sounds crazy, but I have the feeling that I must have had a busy life before now. I just thought I could give the hospital a couple of hours a week and it wouldn't interfere with my work here."

"Okay, I'll check it out on Monday. God knows the hospital can always use help."

"I'd appreciate it."

They finished eating, cleaned up after themselves, then returned to the deck, watching as the stars made a spectacular appearance overhead. Their conversation was light and easy, matching the mildness of the night surrounding them.

Jane released a contented sigh and looked up at the stars. "My mother used to tell me that every time two people fell in love, God put a new star in the sky. She'd say, 'Just look, sugarplum, look at all the stars . . . all the love that's in this world.'" Jane felt a sudden fullness in her throat at the abrupt memory, and the blanket of stars she'd been staring at blurred into a mist of unexpected tears.

It was there like a gift, a clear vision of her mother. Jane mentally grasped it to her, the heart-shaped face topped by gray curls, the spicy scent of the familiar perfume and the melodic tone of her voice. Jane reached for more, overwhelmed with disappointment when nothing else followed.

"My mother had a slight variation on the theme," Frank said, his voice a deep rumble just audible above the distant crashing waves. "She used to tell me that every time somebody made a wish and it came true, a star appeared."

Jane swallowed the lump in her throat and blinked rapidly to dispel the tears. She held the memory of her mother close for a moment longer, realizing whatever had prompted it was gone.

"Are some of those stars your wishes?" she asked, as she pulled her gaze from the sky to the man sitting next to her.

He didn't answer for a long moment. "Not many." His voice was deeper, as if the disappointment of wishes unfulfilled burdened it with a heavy weight.

"Which ones aren't there?" she asked, hoping she wasn't prying, but wanting to know.

He turned and looked at her, his dark gaze glittering in the moonlight reflecting off the water. "When I was ten, I wished for a horse. That one didn't get a star."

Jane smiled. "I think nine out of ten children didn't get that particular star hung in the heavens."

"I also wished for a brother or a sister, but I didn't get that one, either." His mouth turned upward. "But I suppose I should have taken that wish to my parents."

Jane laughed. "Yes, it would seem they were probably in control of making that one come true."

His gaze returned to the diamond-studded sky. For a long moment, they were both silent, captured by the beauty overhead. "I wanted children," he said. The words, spoken so starkly, so devoid of emotion hung for a moment in the air, startling Jane in their simple need.

"You can still hang that particular star," she said softly.

He shook his head. "No. I'm thirty-five years old and far too settled in my ways to think of a wife or a family. I've got a full life. There's no time or energy for a woman or children." There was a finality to his voice and he turned away. Jane realized he regretted giving her that personal piece of himself.

Still, the unfulfilled wish touched her deeply. She studied his features in the lunar light, seeing there the strength of character, the lines that empathy had etched in his face.

She felt a sad regret for him, and the children he would never have. She knew instinctively that he would have made a good father. His love for his children would have been tempered with strength and patience.

For a moment, she had a clear mental image of Frank walking along the beach, a toddler at his side. She could almost hear his murmuring voice as he told the child of the ocean, and the stars, of life.

Children . . . babies. The pleasant image was suddenly usurped by a terrifying one. Her head filled with the mournful sound from her nightmare . . . the horrifying cries of a terrified infant . . . the flames that smelled of smoke and death . . . the blood that stained her hands.

She closed her eyes, shivering despite the warmth of the night. Why did the vision fill her with such terror, and worse . . . such guilt?

A helpless sense of despair swept through her as she wondered what it all meant and what it had to do with her. Before Frank had found her lying unconscious on the beach, what had she done?

What had she done?

Chapter 7

Jane stood precariously balanced on a chair as she reached for the end of the curtain rod. As she stretched outward, the chair tipped and she gasped, struggling to regain her balance.

"Jane!" Frank's strong hands clasped her around the waist, steadying her as she took a deep breath to still her rapid heartbeats. He helped her down from the chair, his hands lingering at her waist. "Are you all right?"

She nodded and took a deep breath. "I just lost my balance for a moment."

He stepped back as if he suddenly realized there was no longer any reason to hold her. "What were you doing?"

"I thought I'd get those curtains down and clean the windows this morning."

"But it's Saturday."

She smiled at him. "Have I forgotten some sort of federal or state law, or something...that nobody cleans windows on Saturday?"

He laughed. "No, no state or federal violation. It's merely your employer's wish that you do not wash windows today."

She was gratified that the pleasantness that had marked their evening the night before obviously extended into this morning. "And what is it that my employer would like for me to do?" She continued to smile up at him, enjoying the warmth of his eyes.

"I think we should spend the day outside on the beach, enjoying the sand, the sun, the water and perhaps a picnic lunch." He frowned as she walked past him and into the kitchen. "Jane...wait...what are you doing?"

She smiled teasingly. "I'm going to make our picnic lunch."

As she packed a cooler full of sandwiches and goodies, drinks and fruit, she realized she was looking forward too much to spending the day with Frank. It almost scared her, the breathless sort of anticipation that accompanied her lunch preparation. It confused her, the warmth and pleasure she got when she was in his company. Yes, it confused her, but left her wanting more.

And something equally confusing was the fact that when the chair had pitched beneath her and the world had momentarily gone topsy-turvy, she'd experienced a strong feeling of déjà vu. The sensation was so powerful that for a moment she had felt nauseated. She searched for a meaning to this in vain.

Then, she shoved these thoughts aside, deciding she was just going to take this day as a gift. It would be a day in which she would not dwell on the mystery of her past. She refused to speculate on what the future would bring. Today she just wanted to be a normal woman spending time with an attractive man.

Minutes later, they left the house. Frank carried the cooler and a blanket, and Jane toted a beach ball and an umbrella. The sun was already hot even though it was just after ten o'clock.

As Frank spread out the blanket, Jane watched him in appreciation. With his muscle T-shirt and cutoff jean shorts, he looked more like a rugged beach bum than a professional man. Only the beeper he pulled out of his pocket attested to the fact that he was other than a devil-may-care surfer.

She watched as he slathered on sunscreen, then handed her the bottle.

A bit self-consciously, Jane pulled her T-shirt over her head, leaving her clad only in the new blue bathing suit. She quickly applied the sunscreen.

"You know it's not that bad," he observed.

She looked at him blankly, then blushed, realizing she'd been touching the scar on the side of her neck. "It's just strange to have something like this and not know how you got it."

"Perhaps the scar has something to do with what happened to you, with what brought on the amnesia. It doesn't look that old."

"Perhaps," she agreed thoughtfully. She stretched out on the blanket, not wanting to think about the fire that haunted her dreams. She didn't want the day tainted with those ugly visions.

She was conscious of him pulling off his shirt and positioning himself next to her on the blanket. She was intensely aware of his body heat radiating down her side, as hot as the sun's rays overhead. She remained still for several minutes, simply enjoying the warmth that surrounded her.

"Did you know that right here on this very beach was where I received my first kiss?"

Jane rolled over on her side and propped herself on an elbow. "What was her name?"

"Sara. She had bouncing red curls and a face full of freckles, and I thought she was the most wonderful girl alive." He smiled reflectively. "We were sitting on the beach after swimming and her hair was all frizzy around her face. Her nose was peeling and she smelled like peanut butter. I thought she was the most gorgeous girl I'd ever seen."

Jane smiled, able to visualize the two innocent children sitting on the beach. "How old were you?"

He grinned. "Thirty-three. It was just last year."

She slapped his shoulder playfully. "I'm serious," she protested as he rumbled a laugh.

"I was ten. She was an older woman ... twelve if I remember correctly. Her family moved that summer."

Jane lay back down, closing her eyes against the brightness of the sun. "Those are the kind of memories I think I miss the most," she said softly.

"You mean childhood ones?" he asked.

"No, not specifically childhood ones. Just the memories that make you feel warm and fuzzy inside whenever you pull them out and examine them. You know, the Hallmark-moment kind of memories."

"Sooner or later, they'll come back. Sooner or later, they'll all come back."

After a few minutes of silence, she realized Frank had fallen asleep. She could tell by his deep, even breathing, the complete lack of tension in his body. The man was obviously exhausted and she knew it had to be from the hours he kept. He was nothing short of a workaholic and she wondered what demons drove him to keep up the frantic pace.

She rolled onto her side and took the opportunity to fully study him while in his vulnerable state. His eyelashes were sinfully dark, decadently long for a man. What would they feel like flickering softly against her neck? she wondered.

His mouth was nicely formed, with a full bottom lip that caused her to remember that single moment when she'd tasted it. She'd liked the taste of his mouth, had lost herself momentarily to the sensual connection despite the brevity of the kiss.

Apparently, he hadn't shaved that morning for a faint shadow of whiskers covered the lower portion of his face. They were dark, but glinted with auburn highlights as the sun stroked each one. She knew they would be erotically coarse against her skin.

Stop it, she chided herself, rolling over onto her back and squeezing her eyes tightly closed. It was silly to fantasize about making love to Frank, ridiculous to even consider the possibility of a relationship with him. After all, he was the one who'd said he had no time or energy for a woman in his life.

Besides, what did she have to offer to anyone right now? Pieces of memories that made no sense, portions of a life she couldn't remember, a name that didn't even belong to her? No matter how attracted she was to Frank, without her memories, she couldn't truly give to him what he deserved.

She released a deep sigh. Until she reclaimed her past, she didn't have much of anything to offer anyone. She was stuck in a strange sort of limbo, her entire life on hold.

She looked back at Frank, wishing she had her memories, that she was whole enough to plunge ahead and explore the emotions that he stirred in her. There was something there...something growing between them daily. It was a strange sort of intimacy, an attraction that increased in intensity daily, a desire that flourished despite her struggle against it.

She brushed away a strand of hair from her neck, the tips of her fingers lingering on the taut scar along the lower portion of her neck. Even though she'd tried and tried to tell herself that the terrifying nightmares and visions were nothing but figments of her imagination, deep inside she knew differently. They were memories, and the scar that marked the side of her neck was the result of the horrifying fire that haunted her. She knew it with a certainty that followed no reason. She also knew that, until she remembered who she was, *what* she had done, she had no right to get involved with anyone.

She felt Frank stir next to her and she looked over at him, smiling as she saw that he'd awakened. He sat up and grinned sheepishly. "Whew, I went out like a light. How long was I asleep?"

"Not very long... just a few minutes."

"It must be the heat."

"Hmm, it wouldn't have anything to do with the fact that you work too hard," she observed wryly.

"I like my work," he retorted.

"I think you're obsessed with it," Jane returned lightly.

He shrugged. "Perhaps," he agreed, his gaze going out toward the water. "Do you swim?"

Jane frowned thoughtfully. "I don't know. I think I must because the water doesn't frighten me. In fact, it looks very inviting."

He stood up and held out his hand to her. "Then let's go."

She hesitated a moment, then placed her hand in his, laughing as he tugged her toward the water with the enthusiasm of a young boy. He didn't hesitate at the edge of the water, but plunged forward, attempting to pull Jane in with him. As the waves licked at her feet and ankles, she squealed with shock and halted. "It's so cold," she protested, pulling back, reluctant to enter any farther.

"You'll get used to it." Frank laughed and tugged her once again.

"Let me just ease myself in," she exclaimed, digging her toes into the sand like a recalcitrant crab.

"That's the coward's way." His eyes sparkled with a youthful merriment and his hand tightened around hers. "Don't think about it, as they say in the commercials, just do it."

Jane laughed and nodded her head. "Okay." She squealed again as he pulled her farther into the water.

As a huge wave swept over them, engulfed them, she surfaced sputtering and laughing, wrapped in Frank's strong arms.

"Okay?" he asked, his arms a firm anchor against the crashing water.

She nodded, unable to speak for a moment, overwhelmed with tactile sensations as the buoyancy of the water guided her body intimately against his. Her hands held on to the strength of his shoulders, her legs molded to the firm length of his.

She was disappointed when he released her and she found herself treading water. "You can swim," he proclaimed.

She took a few experimental strokes, then smiled at him, noting how the water clung to his gorgeous eyelashes. "I guess it's like riding a bicycle—once you learn, you never forget."

"Come on, I'll race you." He took off, swimming away from the shoreline toward the calmer waters on the other side of the waves. After only a moment's hesitation, Jane followed, stroking hard until she was right beside him. He slowed his pace and for a few lengths they swam side by side in synchronized rhythm.

Like lovers in a water dance, their motions mirrored each other, creating a feeling of intimacy, of togetherness despite the fact they didn't touch. This must be what it's like to make love, she thought, matching her movements to his. The water surrounded her, caressed her body...the same water that surrounded and caressed his. This thought only further increased the illusion of intimacy. She wondered if their hearts beat with the same rhythm as their bodies moved in mirrored motion.

"Still cold?" he asked, breaking his stroke and once again treading water.

"No, it feels wonderful." She pushed her wet hair away from her forehead and raised her face toward the sun.

"Do you know how to bodysurf?" he asked.

"I don't think so."

He grinned in boyish invitation. "Want to learn?"

"Why not?" she readily agreed, deciding she'd do anything to keep that appealing smile on his lips, that enthusiastic expression on his face.

For the next hour, they frolicked like dolphins, their laughter competing with the sound of the waves and the cries of the gulls overhead. Frank was patient in teaching her the art of bodysurfing and cheered lustily as she successfully rode a wave all the way to the sandy beach. They played a childish game of tag, took turns dunking each other and played catch with the colorful beach ball.

By noon, they were back on the blanket, ravenous and exhausted. Frank put up the umbrella, casting welcome shade against the unrelenting heat. As Jane got out the food, he watched her, enjoying the kiss of sunshine that brightened her cheeks with color.

Despite her thinness, the blue bathing suit she wore emphasized her femininity, showing off the rounded curves of her breasts, the slight flare of her hips. With her long hair flowing down her back and drying in the light wind, she looked like a mythical mermaid whose siren song could lead him back into the depths of the sea forever.

He forced his attention away from her and to his sandwich, confused by the emotions that swept over him. She was getting to him. Without being aware of it, apparently without even trying, she was definitely getting under his skin. And he didn't know what to do about it. And more frightening than that, he wasn't sure he wanted to do anything about it.

"Penny for your thoughts," she said as she shoved a strand of her hair away from her face and took a bite of her sandwich.

He smiled, pushing his disturbing thoughts out of his mind. He didn't want to worry about where he was headed, he only wanted to enjoy his present place and time. "They aren't worth a penny."

"Hmm, the sun and the water do that to you, drive every meaningful thought straight out of your head."

"Yes, but it's nice, isn't it?" Again he observed how beautiful she looked. The sun had splashed color on her face and brought freckles to the surface of the skin on her shoulders. "You better be careful that you don't get too much sun," he said. "It wouldn't take much for you to get a nasty burn."

She poked at her cheeks, then at the tip of her nose, wincing slightly. "I think I'd better play it safe and spend the rest of the day under the umbrella."

They made short order of the lunch Jane had packed. He watched indulgently as she took half a sandwich and crumbled it into pieces, then threw it to the more bold of the birds who approached their blanket.

"I think I'll swim a little bit more," he said as she rejoined him beneath the shade of the umbrella. She nodded and stretched out on the blanket, closing her eyes, a soft smile still curving her lips.

Frank looked at her for a long moment, wondering if she had any idea how provocative she looked even when completely relaxed.

He could see the swell of her breasts above the neckline of her bathing suit, the wispy waist he thought he could span with his hands. He could almost imagine those long legs locked around his back, holding him against her with fiery strength. More than anything now, he wanted to gather her into his arms, watch her eyes flutter open in surprise, then darken as she welcomed his desire. He wanted to taste again those lips that had entranced him so completely, feel her heated body moving wildly against his own—

He rose from the blanket and raced toward the water, diving into the waves and swimming strongly, his physical exertions dousing the heat rushing through his veins.

Soon the inner heat was gone and he relaxed, rolling over on his back and floating. He'd forgotten how much he loved the water. It had been too long since he'd taken a day just to enjoy himself.

Before Jane, he'd spent most of his days off either at his office catching up on paperwork or at the clinic volunteering away his free time. But he hadn't considered doing either of those things this morning. He'd thought only of spending the day on the beach with Jane.

Who was she? Where had she come from? What events had brought her here? He wanted her to remember, needed to know where she belonged. He was afraid to go forward, follow through on the obvious attraction that existed between them without knowing about her life, what she would eventually go back to. He'd thought the past didn't matter once before, and the end result had been devastating.

He couldn't go through the same kind of pain he'd experienced with Gloria. He wouldn't. He was better off maintaining a platonic relationship with Jane, and knew he must not allow it to deepen into anything more. He'd keep focused on his work, the endless hours of need he filled for others. That was his place in the big scheme of things.

Jane, filling his house with life, waiting up for him no matter how late he got home. The contentment that filled him when he walked in the front door and smelled her presence all around him...these were just momentary respites from reality. He could enjoy them, but had to realize they weren't lasting. Eventually she'd be gone. He couldn't let himself forget that.

He rolled over and looked toward the shoreline, surprised to see Jane on her feet and motioning for him. Sensing an urgency in her posture, he swam quickly in and ran toward her.

"This thing went off," she explained, holding out his beeper.

"I'll have to call in. They would only beep me if there was an emergency." He hesitated as he looked at their stuff that littered the blanket.

"Go on," Jane instructed. "Go make your call. I'll gather this stuff together and take it back."

Hesitating only a moment longer, Frank ran toward the house.

Jane gathered their things, disappointment briefly flaring inside her. If there was an emergency, then the odds were good that Frank would leave. Even though she knew it was his job, that it was a part of who he was, she couldn't help but feel a certain amount of disappointment that their day together would end.

By the time she reached the house Frank met her at the back door, already changed into slacks and a dress shirt. "I've got to get to the hospital," he said, sitting down at the table so he could put on his socks and shoes. "There's been an accident...a busload of people and a semitruck."

"Oh no." Jane shivered, her mind suddenly filled with a hellish vision of death. The vision intensified and claimed her mind like an unwanted hallucination. She was there, in the center of it all. She was a participant in a drama she didn't understand, couldn't comprehend. For a split second, she was lost to the chaos of her thoughts.

"Jane." Frank's sharp tone brought her back and she stared at him blankly. "Are you all right?"

"Yes...yes, I'm fine." She took a deep breath to steady herself. "You'd better hurry. They'll need you." She walked him to the door.

"I don't know when I'll be home," he said.

"It's okay. I'll just expect you when I see you," Jane replied.

He nodded absently. He leaned over and kissed her on the cheek, then hurried toward his car. She remained at the front door until he was out of sight, then she turned and went back inside.

She reached up and touched the spot where his lips had touched her. She knew the gesture had been unconscious on his part, that he probably didn't even realize he'd done it. But he had, and for just a moment, she had felt like a wife. And for that single moment...it had been wonderful.

Frank sat in his car, his hands tightly gripping the steering wheel as the dawn light crept over the horizon. He needed to go inside. He needed to get some sleep. The past twelve hours had been pure hell.

Exhaustion burned his eyes, clogged his throat. He swallowed convulsively, trying to think of something, anything other than the patients he had struggled to save.

With a deep sigh, he got out of his car and went inside, surprised to find the kitchen light on and what smelled like a fresh pot of coffee. The early-morning light streaming in the window painted the room in lush gold tones, and for a moment, Frank leaned wearily against the wall, wanting the gold light to fill him up, remove the black hole in his heart.

"Oh, there you are," Jane said from behind him.

He whirled around, his emotions too close to the surface, his hold on them too tenuous. He didn't want to see her. He didn't want to have to talk to anyone at all. "What are you doing still up?" he snapped, strangely irritated by her presence.

Her eyes blinked in surprise. "I'm not 'still' up," she replied calmly as she moved past him into the kitchen. She reached into the cabinet and pulled out two mugs, then filled them with coffee. "I woke up about an hour ago and let the dogs out, then realized you hadn't come home yet. I couldn't go back to sleep and thought perhaps when you *did* get home, you would appreciate some coffee."

As she set the mugs at the table and sat down, Frank felt his anger whoosh out of him, leaving only a deep, consuming sorrow behind.

He sat down at the table and wrapped his hands around the mug, wishing the warmth would broadcast itself through his entire body.

"Bad, huh?" Jane's gaze studied him intently and he merely nodded, not quite meeting her eyes. He was afraid that beneath the intensity of those sea-green pools, he would crumble, expose himself as weak and needy.

"Want to talk about it?" she asked softly, her hand reaching out to enfold his.

To his horror, he felt the sudden dampness of tears seeking escape. They pressed hotly behind his eyes and in desperation he stood up, bumping the table and sloshing coffee over the sides of his cup. "Damn," he raged, grabbing for a roll of paper towels on top of the counter.

"Let me," she said as she gently took the towels from him and cleaned up the mess.

Frank sank back into the chair and buried his face in his hands, shuddering with the effort of trying to control the emotions that threatened to erupt.

"Frank...talk to me." Her hands touched his shoulders, lingering there to offer support, comfort. And suddenly he wanted her comfort. The grief that tore at his insides was too much to hold in. With a groan of desperation, he turned in the chair and leaned into her. Her arms enfolded him against her warmth and sweet scent and Frank allowed his tears to burn hotly down his cheeks.

He didn't know how long she held him, not saying a word. She simply stroked his hair and held him tightly. She was his asylum against the anguish, his sanctuary against the inadequacies that mocked him. He buried his head in her midsection and surrendered completely to his grief.

Jane let him cry, touched deeply by his gut-wrenching sobs. He was a little boy needing comfort, an awkward teen needing reassurance, a man needing love. Suddenly she knew she wanted to be all . . . everything for him. She somehow recognized the deep despair that gripped him, recognized it and wanted to take it from him. She wanted to shoulder his pain as he had shouldered hers the night she'd found out she wasn't really Jane Smith.

She held him until his deep sobs subsided and he finally pushed away from her. He stood up and walked across the room, his back rigidly facing her. "Three . . ." His voice was deep with strain and mourning. "I lost three children. It was a busload of kids on their way to the zoo. Most of them escaped serious injuries, but three of them were bad. I worked and worked, but I couldn't save them. . . ." His voice broke on the last word and his shoulders sagged forward.

"Frank." She moved to stand just behind him, tugging on one of his arms to turn him around to face her. She reached up and placed her hands on either side of his face. "You're not God. You can't save them all."

He stared at her with pain-filled eyes, eyes that radiated a deep soul-torment. "But they were so tiny... just beginning their lives. I... I wanted to save them so badly."

"And you didn't do everything possible to do that?" she asked.

"Of course, I did," he retorted with a trace of indignation. He closed his eyes for a moment and her hands softly caressed the sides of his whisker roughened cheeks. "I did everything I possibly could." This time his voice held a weary resignation. When he opened his eyes once again, the grief was still there, but the deep torment was gone. "I did all that was humanly possible."

She nodded, her hands still stroking his face, wiping away the remnants of his tears. "And you are only human."

"Yes...yes...only human." His arms closed around her, drawing her closer, and his eyes darkened with a different emotion, one Jane recognized and welcomed.

She parted her lips as his descended downward, claiming hers in a kiss that stole her breath away. The kiss wasn't tentative or hesitant; it was hot and demanding as his tongue flicked against hers.

His arms encircled her as if to pull her into him, through him, and she melted, loving the intimacy of his body so close to hers.

His mouth was dark magic creating tiny flames of fire as his lips nipped behind her ear, then down her neck. Jane knew it was need as much as desire that prompted his passion, the need to connect with life after the hours of fighting against death. She didn't care what prompted the passion, she only accepted all that he offered, dropping her head back to allow him access to the hollow of her neck.

His hands moved up and down her back, evoking tingling heat within her as his mouth once again claimed hers. Jane clung to him, tangling her hands in the richness of his hair, molding her body intimately against the masculine lines of his.

As his mouth plied hers, she realized this was what she had wanted from the moment he'd taken her out of that horrid rental cottage and brought her into his home. She wanted to belong to him. She didn't care if it was just momentary...she didn't care if it was just in a physical manner. She wanted him to make love to her and banish the sense of isolation that clutched at her heart.

She moaned deep in the back of her throat as his hands moved from her back, around to cup the fullness of her breasts. She could feel the heat of his caress even through the light cotton blouse and the lacy bra.

"Frank..." She stepped back just enough to take one of his hands in hers. She led him through the kitchen and down the hallway toward her bedroom.

"Wait." He hesitated just outside her door, staring at her as if he'd just resurfaced from a dream and wasn't sure exactly where he was. "This isn't right...we can't do this," he said tentatively.

"It's okay. I...I want to." Jane's face flushed at her own boldness.

He smiled gently, his gaze tender. He swept a strand of her hair away from her face, then dropped his hands to his sides. "Jane, if we make love now, it will only complicate things for you. We don't know who you are, where you've come from..." He paused a long moment, then added softly, "Who might be waiting for you."

He leaned forward and pressed his lips lightly against her forehead. "Thank you for being here for me. I needed..." He paused for a moment. "You helped me through what would have been an even rougher time than it was."

Jane nodded, disappointment welling up in her throat, but knowing the moment for abandonment had passed. He touched her cheek one last time, then with a tired sigh, he turned and disappeared into his own room, closing the door behind him.

She walked toward the kitchen, her body still tingling from his caresses, her insides still aflame from the sheer hunger in his kisses. She poured herself a cup of coffee, then stepped outside on the deck.

The sun peeked over the horizon, promising another hot, cloudless day. Another day of limbo. Another day of blankness. Frustration gnawed inside, like an insidious parasite. She needed to regain her memory. She wanted to know who she was. She wanted more than a name... She wanted the memories to go with the name.

Before she'd wanted to remember for herself, but now she wanted to remember for Frank. She knew now that if she was ever going to know the experience of making love with him, building on the attraction that sparked between them, she had to remember who she was. She absolutely had to.

Chapter 8

"All you need to do is push this cart into the rooms and see if any of the patients want a magazine or a book to read," Etta Maxwell instructed Jane on Monday morning. "Mostly your job is to cheer up whoever you can." She cast Jane a harassed smile as somebody down the hall called for her. "When you're finished taking the book cart around, come back to me and we'll find something else for you to do." The older woman smiled reassuringly and patted Jane's arm. "Don't worry, you'll be fine. Most of the patients are always happy to see the magazine lady." With a wave, Etta hurried down the hallway, her rubber-soled shoes squeaking at her brisk pace.

The "magazine lady." Jane smiled at the official new title as she pushed the cumbersome cart down the hospital corridor. Jane Smith, the magazine lady. At least for the moment she had a definitive identity of sorts. She pushed the cart into the first room and smiled brightly at the two female patients. "Good morning," she greeted them. "Would either of you like a magazine to read?"

"I'd like a bath...that's what I'd like," the older patient exclaimed peevishly. "But those doctors won't let me do nothing...won't even let me leave this dang-fool bed to do my private business." She glared at Jane with faded blue eyes, as if Jane herself was personally responsible for the denial of bathroom privileges.

"I'm sure the doctors know what's best for you," Jane replied smoothly. "Why don't you let me plump up those pillows behind you and find you a good magazine to read."

"Hmm, I suppose," the woman replied grudgingly.

As Jane rearranged the pillows, she was struck by a strange sense of déjà vu, not unlike the one that had hit her so hard when she'd bobbed atop the chair on Saturday morning. It was just a fleeting perception, leaving her bewildered as to what it meant.

It took her all morning to make the rounds of the patient rooms. Although Garett Beach Memorial Hospital was relatively small, there seemed to be a slower pace, a sort of relaxed atmosphere she hadn't felt in a hospital before.

Had she worked in a hospital once? Had she been a nurse? No, somehow that just didn't feel right. She was pretty sure she had no medical knowledge whatsoever.

She was still considering this observation when she shoved the magazine cart back to the storage closet where it belonged.

"So, how's Garett Memorial's newest and prettiest volunteer doing?"

She turned and smiled with pleasure at Frank. "Wonderful. It feels good to be doing something, even if it's just distributing magazines to bored patients."

"Ah, but here at Garett Memorial that's an important job. We pride ourselves on patient morale, and work hard to make them feel pampered and important."

"I was just thinking about that," Jane said. "I was thinking that this seems much more friendly and slower-paced than the hospitals I've been in." She smiled wistfully. "Another clue to the mystery of Jane Smith. I guess I've been in a hospital someplace before this one."

"Well, I've come to take the mystery lady to lunch." He grinned at her. "It's always a good idea to have a doctor around when you eat in the hospital cafeteria."

She laughed at his joke, relieved that she felt no awkwardness, no tension radiating from him. He'd slept most of the day yesterday, then spent the evening hours with his nose in a book. They'd ridden to the hospital together that morning, but he had been quiet, distracted, and she'd worried that somehow, some way, a line had been crossed. A line that would make it impossible to go back to the comfortable companionship they had shared before that moment of vulnerability and brief passion.

However, as he took her elbow and guided her toward the elevator, his smile was warm and relaxed, and she expelled a sigh of relief.

"You look like you're enjoying yourself," he observed as they rode the elevator down.

"I am. As I said, it feels good to be doing something worthwhile."

One of his dark eyebrows danced upward. "Keeping my house in order isn't worthwhile?"

"Yes, but this is different." She grinned up at him. "It feels good to be doing something to help a lot of people instead of helping out just one messy doctor."

He cast her a mock frown. "Messy doctor? I think you've already spent too much time around Etta. She has no respect, either."

As they made their way down the cafeteria line, Jane started to reach for the meat loaf, but stopped as Frank shook his head. "Tastes like dog food," he whispered, making her giggle. She reached for a bowl of Jell-O squares, laughing again as he rolled his eyes. "Colored rubber," he announced. "Your best bet is to stick with the sandwiches and potato chips."

"No wonder you're always ravenous when you get home," she teased.

"I spoke with Harry Wilton about you this morning," he said as they sat down at one of the empty tables. "Because it's not an emergency, he won't be able to see you for another week or two. Since he's been on vacation, he's backlogged right now.''

"I'm ready whenever he is,'' Jane said, disappointed that she'd have to wait that length of time to get started on any therapy that might help her remember.

"In the meantime, he had a suggestion for you. He said you should get a notebook and keep a daily log of all the isolated fragments of memory that surface.''

She nodded. "I'll pick up a notebook from the gift shop this afternoon before I leave.''

"And Etta's taking you home?'' he asked.

"She gets off at two and said it would be no problem to drop me off at your place on the days I work.'' Jane laughed suddenly.

"What's so funny?''

"Etta. She's quite a character. You should have seen her wrestling the nurse-call buzzer away from a patient this morning.''

Frank grinned. "I'll bet it was the patient in room 402. He's our resident curmudgeon. Each morning, he pushes that buzzer until Etta comes and takes it away from him.''

Although the sandwich was dry and tasteless and the chips stale, it was one of the best lunches Jane could ever remember eating, and she knew it was because of Frank.

He chattered like a man who'd been quiet for too long, telling her about his morning rounds and his favorite patients. When he grew silent, she knew he was remembering those patients he'd lost. It thrilled her just a little, the fact that she was growing to know him well enough to read his thoughts, his silences.

"You've got to remember all those you save," she said softly.

He looked at her in surprise, then nodded in agreement. As he launched into another humorous tale, she smiled, enjoying the animation of his face as he shared his experiences.

Again she thought of what a waste it was that he had chosen to live his life alone, without a soul mate.

What had happened that had prompted him to make that particular decision? What event in his past had caused him to close himself off to the notion of love and marriage? But he has reached out once, she reminded herself. He'd reached out to Gloria and something had happened, something that made him decide never to try again.

And yet, as she thought of the previous morning, when his kiss had burned her lips, when she'd seen the desire in his eyes, she knew that he'd been reaching out for her. It was only fear of what she didn't know that had kept him rational and in control.

If only she had her memories back, and if only those memories had nothing in them to keep her and Frank from being together. If only...

"Jane? Are you remembering something?"

"No." She flushed, grateful that he wasn't a mind reader. "No, I'm sorry. I guess I just zoned out for a moment."

"I'm probably boring you to death!" Frank exclaimed.

"Oh, no," she hurriedly protested. "You could never, ever bore me to death." She reached over and enfolded his hand in hers. "I love to listen to you, no matter what you're talking about."

For a moment, their gazes remained locked, and Jane had a feeling their hearts were somehow saying what their lips weren't ready to.

He broke the eye contact and pulled his hand away, and once again she realized whatever it was that kept Frank's heart guarded hadn't diminished in strength. "We'd better get you back or Etta will have me arrested for kidnapping her new help."

Together they left the cafeteria and walked back toward the elevator. "What's Etta got you doing this afternoon?"

"She said something about going over to pediatrics and reading some stories to the kids."

"You should enjoy that." He paused at the elevator door. "I've got to go down to the lab. I'll see you at the house this evening." As she disappeared into the elevator, he turned and walked toward the lab, trying to ignore the warmth that still tingled in his hand from where she had held it.

Every minute he spent with her, he grew more and more confused. She made him remember all the things he'd once dreamed about . . . all the dreams his bout with Gloria had killed.

He shook his head, dismissing thoughts of Jane and whispers of dreams she evoked. He had patients waiting for test results, illnesses needing to be treated. Jane, and the curious warmth she evoked in him, was just another illness he'd medicate until the symptoms were gone. And the best medicine in this case was to stay busy and maintain control.

Hopefully, Harry would be able to get Jane tapped into her memories. She would learn who she was and then she would be gone, out of his house, leaving behind only a tiny ache in his heart. Somehow, this didn't make him feel any better. It simply made him feel worse.

Jane pulled her nightgown over her head and picked up the hairbrush, stifling a yawn as she walked over to the dresser mirror. What a week, she thought as she pulled the brush through her long hair. She was exhausted. She'd worked at the hospital three days, then washed curtains and windows here at the house. Along with the physical activity, she'd worked her brain to death, trying to remember anything, any little piece of her past that might break the memory block that kept her identity a secret.

She set the brush down and stared at her reflection in the mirror. It was still a stranger's face, but one she had grown accustomed to. She frowned, staring at the face that stared back. Something nagged at her... something important... something about the way she looked.

Her frown deepened as she studied each feature, every pore, trying to get a handle on what bothered her. With a sigh, she picked up her hairbrush once again. But before she could use it again, it struck her. With a tiny gasp, she bent her head forward, studying the center part in her hair. There was about a quarter inch of new growth . . . and it was not the same color. It was lighter . . . much lighter.

A shiver raced up her spine as she realized her hair was dyed. Her natural color was nearly blond . . . a far cry from the dark strands that now covered her head.

Lots of people dye their hair, she thought, moving away from the mirror and climbing into bed. It doesn't mean anything at all, she tried to tell herself. She'd probably just been tired of her hair color and had wanted a change. There was nothing ominous in a woman's dying her hair.

She opened the logbook she'd begun keeping and studied the entries she'd made over the course of the past week. On Monday, she'd remembered her dog's name—Pookie. She also remembered that the memory had struck her as she and Frank had sat on the deck, watching a storm brew in the distance. She smiled, thinking of Frank's confession of his childhood fear of storms. "Now I watch storms to prove to myself that I faced and overcame my fear," he'd said.

Yet when she'd moved closer to him, he'd instantly moved away, and she'd known that unlike his fear of storms, the fear of intimacy, the fear of love, was one he hadn't overcome.

She sighed and turned the page. On Wednesday, she'd remembered an Easter Sunday. She'd been about six years old, and she had easily visualized the blue-and-yellow ruffled dress she'd worn to church. She also remembered that it had been a Methodist service, but these tidbits of information did nothing to forward her search for her identity.

She flipped the pages quickly, frustration eating at her as she reviewed the bits and pieces of her life that she had remembered. They were nothing, absolutely nothing but the benign ones anybody might have.

With a sudden, impotent rage, she threw the notebook across the room, watching in satisfaction as it hit the closet door and fell to the floor.

She slumped back against her pillows and frowned, rubbing the scar on her neck thoughtfully. Funny, she hadn't written the visions down in the journal—the fire, the smoke, the scent of death.

She touched the part in her hair, again overwhelmed with questions, questions and unknown answers that had suddenly taken on ominous auras. Why had she been using an alias while staying at those cottages? Why was her hair dyed? To change her appearance? Only people in hiding used fake names and changed their looks. People in hiding . . . or criminals.

She leaned over and turned out her bedroom light, not wanting to think anymore, too exhausted and too frightened to mentally wrestle with the secrets of her past. She released a deep sigh and closed her eyes.

Fire. It seethed around her with a life of its own. Burning...searing...scorching first her face, then her lungs as she breathed in the black smoke that swirled around her.

A baby screamed somewhere nearby, the sound punctuated by a man's whimpering moans. Stop it, she wanted to cry, but no sound emitted from her throat.

She stared down at her hands...hands covered with soot and the glittering wetness of blood. Fear rippled through her, fluttering her heart as tears stung her eyes.

The fire seemed to grow hotter, more intense, and she became aware of the acrid scent of kerosene. In the distance, sirens wailed a warning of their impending approach.

She had to...she had to what? She had to run...get away. Hysterical tears clogged her throat as effectively as the heavy black smoke. At that moment, a figure burst through the flames...a human torch sending out a thin wail of pain. The tears that clogged her throat gave way to screams.

Somebody was shaking her shoulders, shaking her with a force that threatened to dislodge her head from her body. She resurfaced from her horror slowly, becoming aware of first the bedroom, and then Frank shaking her shoulders, repeating her name over and over again.

"Jane...Jane...it's a nightmare," he said, his face lined with concern. "Wake up. You're all right, it's just a nightmare."

She blinked her eyes rapidly, then clutched him around the neck, needing his presence, his reality to remove her from her nightmares of death and destruction. "Just hold me," she whispered, tears still coursing down her cheeks. "Just hold me tight."

He did just that, wrapping his arms firmly around her and drawing her into the strength of his bare chest. Jane squeezed her eyes tightly closed, wanting to lose herself in his heat, wanting to dwell forever in the safety of his arms.

"Want to talk about it?" he asked, his hand stroking her hair.

She shook her head and tightened her embrace around his neck. She didn't want to talk about it, she didn't even want to think about the horrifying images that haunted her sleep. She just wanted to forget them. She wanted Frank's embrace to banish them from her mind forever.

"Jane..." He attempted to pull back from her, but she refused to allow him any distance.

She burrowed more deeply against the heat of his chest, the patch of dark hair tickling her nose. "Please don't go...not yet. Stay here with me a little longer."

"Here, you lie down and I'll stay here until you go back to sleep." He gently extricated himself from her embrace and eased her back against the pillows.

The brilliant moonlight streaming through the window painted him boldly. The silvery light caressed the firm planes of his chest, and pulled shimmering glints out of the silk material of his pajama bottoms.

Jane felt a restless heat stirring inside her and knew that sleep was the furthest thing from her mind. The visions from her nightmare were fading, being replaced by other images—erotic ones that grew in strength as each moment passed.

Frank sat on the very edge of her mattress, looking uncomfortable, a peculiar tension radiating from him. She reached out and took his hand in one of hers. With her other hand, she softly stroked the back of his, outlining each finger with a feather-light touch.

She wasn't afraid anymore. She didn't need him to chase away the black remnants of her dreams any longer. But she needed him for a much different reason.

She sat up once again, not releasing her hold on his hand. She could see the curious expression on his face, a curiosity that didn't quite mask the tension underneath.

"What's the matter?" he asked. "Do you want to talk?"

She shook her head. "No, I don't want to talk." She leaned forward until she could feel his breath on her face, fancied she could hear the rapid beating of his heart. "I want..." She swallowed the last of her sentence, pressing her mouth against his, instead.

He hesitated, holding himself still and unyielding against her insistent mouth. Then, with a soft groan of acquiescence, he kissed her back. His mouth moved hungrily against hers, his tongue delving inside to fill her up with icy fire that sent delicious shivers of anticipation down her spine.

She placed her hands on the back of his head and gently urged him forward until he was next to her on the bed, his body prone with hers. Still their mouths remained fused, transferring heat and emotion to each other, feeding on each other's desire.

She leaned into him and pressed her breasts against the expanse of his chest, her nipples hardening in response to the evocative heat and the erotic roughness of his chest hair. With her body so close to his, she could feel his heartbeat, erratic and pounding, matching the primitive rhythm of her own.

She remembered that moment when they had been swimming together, when she had imagined that it was like making love. Now she realized it wasn't. Synchronized swimming couldn't begin to match the wonder, the passion, the intense nonverbal communication that came with making love.

And at the moment, she and Frank were definitely communicating. His lips whispered to her of his passion. His hands splayed against her back murmured of his tenuous hold on his control...a control Jane wanted to snap.

She moved one of her hands, placing it on the upper portion of his thigh. She could feel the heat of his flesh, the taut muscle beneath the coolness of the silky material.

He inhaled sharply as she moved her hand up the firmness of his thigh, across his lower stomach, lingering lightly on the slight protrusion of his hipbone.

With another soft groan, his hands moved from her back to cover her breasts with his hot palms. His fingertips caressed the hardness of her nipples through the cotton material of her nightgown.

Impatiently, she threw off the sheet that separated them, then pulled her nightgown over her head and tossed it to the floor.

Frank froze, his expression stark in the moon's illumination. He looked tormented, as if he desperately clung to the last of his control. Jane felt his gaze as it lingered like a hot caress on her bare breasts, then his eyes locked with hers, and she saw his inner struggle.

She didn't want to give him an opportunity to think of all the reasons that they shouldn't continue. She didn't want his good sense to rule them. She wanted passion to rule. She wanted to seduce him into madness and follow him there.

She took his hands and placed them on her breasts, whispering his name in an alluring plea. He closed his eyes and shuddered, and when he looked at her again, she saw the flames of desire had replaced the hesitation, passion had overwhelmed common sense.

As his lips covered hers once again, she tasted his surrender and she did the same, releasing herself to the hot winds of pleasure that swept through her as he caressed her breasts, consumed her mouth.

She plucked at the waistband of his pajama bottoms, impatient to feel all of him next to her. This was one place where there was no room for barriers of any kind, whether it be the physical restraint of silk material or the emotional barrier of her lack of a memory.

With an agile motion, he pulled off the pajamas and cast them aside, then moved back against her. Her breath caught in her throat as she felt his rigid arousal against her, recognized the extent of his desire for her.

She moaned and closed her eyes as his lips blazed a trail of heat down her neck, pausing to savor the tip of first one breast, then the other. As his mouth worked its magic, his hand caressed her flat abdomen, down the inside of one thigh. She caught her bottom lip between her teeth as he touched the very core of her, his fingers stroking with feather-light movements that made her want to scream with pleasure.

Finally, she couldn't still the cries of pleasure any longer. Her body was overwhelmed with sensations too exquisite to fight. She was vaguely aware of whimpers escaping her lips as she rode the tidal waves of elation that swept over her.

She was still riding the crest of waves when he settled between her thighs, poised with the tip of his maleness against her yielding heat. Jane opened her eyes and looked up at him, felt herself falling into the fires that burned in the darkness of his eyes.

As he entered her, plunging deep within, she knew with a certainty that she'd never experienced this before. She might have made love in the past, but never had it been this intense, this compelling, this complete.

She locked her legs around his back, pulling him more deeply inside her, arching up to meet each thrust. At first, they moved slowly, languidly, like two long-time lovers who wanted to savor each sensation, every perception. For Jane, it was like making love the very first time, with no expectations, no memories of other men, other loves, to clutter the pureness of the experience.

But soon languor gave way to fierce need and they moved in a frenzy, their bodies covered with a fine sheen of perspiration as they gave in to their incredible hunger.

Jane felt an explosion building inside her, sensed an answering one in him. She could feel him pulsating deep inside her, and with a sob, she allowed the explosion to overtake her, crying his name as he stiffened with his own release.

For a long moment, neither of them moved. They remained joined, their breaths slowing as their hearts resumed a more normal rhythm.

Tears burned in Jane's eyes as her body tingled with its own memory of what had just transpired. She was awed by the experience, moved beyond belief by her overwhelming emotions, the feeling of rightness, the feeling that she belonged.

Frank rolled over to the side, breaking their physical connection, his face turned away from her. He emitted a deep, heavy sigh, one that instantly filled Jane with a horrible sense of dread.

"Frank?" She spoke his name softly, wanting to breach the distance she felt, the emotional barrier she could almost see him rebuilding between them.

He looked at her, his eyes filled with the regret she'd been afraid she'd see. "Please don't," she whispered, placing her hand over his chest.

"Don't what?" His voice sounded detached, remote.

She leaned up on one elbow and looked at him, wishing she could reach inside his chest and grab his heart, hold it captive forever. But she knew he'd already tucked it away where it couldn't be reached. "Don't regret what we just shared."

"Jane, how can I help but regret it. It's madness. It only complicates things for both you and me." He sat up suddenly and reached for his pajama bottoms. In one swift movement, he left the bed and yanked the pants on, then stood staring down at her, remorse once again darkening his eyes.

He muttered an unintelligible curse. "This should never have happened. Sooner or later, you're going to remember where you came from, what kind of life you had. Sooner or later, you might remember somebody who loves you . . . somebody you love."

He raked a hand through his hair, shaking his head in bewilderment. "We can't do this, Jane. Until you remember your past, this can't happen again. We've already crossed a line that will make it difficult to go back, but we can't compound the problem by repeating the mistake."

His eyes blazed with a sudden ferver. "You need to remember, Jane. We can't go forward until you can remember your past." He didn't wait for her to answer; instead, he turned and left her room.

Jane fought the impulse to run after him, knowing someplace deep in her heart that he was right. She rolled onto her back and stared bleakly at the ceiling. Yes, he was right. But there was one small problem. As much as she was growing to care for Frank, as much as she wanted to repeat this beautiful experience again and again, when she thought of those visions from her dreams, the horrifying nightmare she knew was a memory, the bleakness inside her grew. As she contemplated the fact that she had been using an assumed name, that her hair was dyed to disguise its real color... As she relived the overwhelming sense of responsibility and guilt those terrible visions always evoked, she didn't *want* to remember her past. No matter how much she was beginning to care for Frank, she couldn't do it. She didn't want to remember her past at all.

Chapter 9

Frank stood at the window in the doctors' lounge, watching the sun rising in the eastern sky. It was going to be another hot one. Hot and steamy, one of those intensely uncomfortable days Garett Beach suffered throughout the year.

But the physical discomfort couldn't begin to compete with Frank's internal discomfort. Not only had he made a horrible mistake the night before by making love to Jane, he'd compounded the error by running out of the house this morning before she got up.

He'd run like a coward, afraid of what he might see in the liquid depths of her green eyes, afraid of what she'd make him feel.

He rubbed a hand wearily across his forehead. The problem was she'd already made him feel too much.

Even now, a burst of desire swept through him as he thought of the way her long legs had locked around him, pulling him deeper into her heat and moistness.

When he'd first gone into her bedroom, he'd been worried about her. She'd been crying out, the cries alternating with whimpers and screams of terror. He'd only wanted to comfort her. He'd never dreamed things would get so far out of control.

The heat of the sun couldn't even begin to compare with the volley of fire that rocketed through his groin as he remembered the taste of her skin, the soft, satiny texture as he'd caressed her. It had been magic— pure magic—to make love to her.

It had been sheer torture to jump out of that bed, remove himself from her, when all he'd wanted to do was remain beside her through the night hours, awaken with her in his arms.

God must be punishing me, he thought as he moved away from the window and over to the coffee urn. First, he got involved with a woman who'd lied about her past, and now one who couldn't remember her past. "God is definitely punishing me for some evil, youthful transgression," he murmured out loud.

"Ah, it's usually a cop-out to blame the Creator."

Frank whirled around to see Harry Wilton standing behind him. "Problems, Frank?"

"Nothing that I need to pay you to fix," Frank said wryly. "What are you doing here at this time of the morning? I thought psychiatrists kept bankers' hours."

"They admitted a suicide attempt early this morning and needed a psych evaluation." Harry moved over to the coffeepot and helped himself. "It was a teenage girl whose boyfriend broke up with her. She wanted to scare him more than she wanted to hurt herself. Finding a nicer boyfriend will heal her much more quickly than I could." He sat down at the table and gestured for Frank to join him. "I thought today was your day off."

"It is. I just decided to check on a few patients," Frank replied, sitting down at the table. The truth was he'd needed to get out of the house and the hospital was the only place he knew to come to to get his thoughts together. He hadn't been ready to face Jane. He'd needed some distance, some perspective so he could face her and not want her again.

"Actually, I was going to call you this morning, anyway," Harry said, pausing a moment to sip from his cup. "I've got a free hour this afternoon if your friend would like to come in."

Hope flared in Frank's heart. Maybe Harry could help Jane. Maybe he could help her remember if she had a lover, a fiancé... a husband. Even though she maintained she was certain she wasn't married, Frank absolutely couldn't go any further until he knew for certain. "What time?" he asked.

"Two o'clock."

Frank studied the man across from him. He'd heard that Harry was a good psychiatrist, that he was a man who cared intensely about his work. "You think you can help her?"

Harry shrugged his thick shoulders. "I don't know. I'm not going to make you any false promises." He worried the cup between his hands. "I'll be truthful with you, I've never worked with an amnesia victim before. There are no drugs I can prescribe to help her remember, no magic pill she can take that'll instantly bring back her memories."

"What kind of treatment will you try?"

"Word association, picture interpretation... hopefully, something will jiggle the memories loose. In any case, it's going to take some work, and she's going to have to want to remember."

"I'll see that she makes the appointment this afternoon," Frank said.

"Great." Harry drained his coffee and stood up. "And now I think I'll head back home. If I'm lucky, I can get a couple of hours of snooze in before my first official appointment of the day." With a backhanded wave to Frank, he left the doctors' lounge.

Frank stared into the black depths of his coffee cup. He hadn't wanted to get involved with another woman again. His experience with Gloria had left a bitter taste in his mouth.

She'd taken his love, smashed it against the rocky shore and left him bereaved and angry. At that time, he'd made the decision not to trust in love again, not to gamble with his heart.

Then Jane had dropped on his beach and in a moment of weakness and passion, he'd let himself make love to her. He tightened his grip around his coffee cup. Okay, he'd made a mistake, but he'd meant what he'd said to her the night before. He wouldn't repeat the same mistake. He wouldn't even consider going forward in a relationship with Jane until she managed to go backward and reclaim her life. Until that time, he refused to relinquish his heart. Jane had his companionship, his support, and through his own weakness, she had managed to capture his passion, but until she got back her memories, she would never have his heart.

Jane ran along the beach, Mutt and Jeff nipping at her heels, dancing around her like her own personal guardians. It was just after dawn, but already the sun bore down with hot intensity.

When she'd awakened that morning to find Frank still gone, regret had washed over her. She knew she had been in control the night before. She had consciously seduced him, wanting him more than she'd thought possible. Granted, he'd been a willing participant in the seduction, but she knew he'd been right when he'd said an imaginary line had been crossed, one that would make it difficult for them to go back to the easy camaraderie they'd shared before last night.

She didn't want to go back. She wanted to go forward. She wanted to spend her days keeping his house and doing her volunteer work at the hospital. She wanted to spend the evenings listening to him share the events of his day. She wanted to spend her nights wrapped in his arms, safe and warm in the mindless act of love.

She stopped running and leaned over to catch her breath, a stitch in her side telling her she'd pushed herself too hard. She straightened and gazed at the rental cottages in the distance. That was her past. An assumed name and dyed hair was her past. Running...hiding...guilt...*that* was her past. And she didn't want it.

She walked slowly back to the house. She felt as if she'd been reborn when she'd awakened in the hospital without a name. She didn't want to go back and find out what kind of person she'd been, what she might have done. She liked the person she was now. She liked Jane Smith. She knew, with certainty, that she wouldn't like the person she had been and she was deathly afraid to find out what she had done. As much as she cared about Frank, she couldn't go back...not even for him.

The minute she walked into the house, she saw the answering machine flickering the red light that signaled a message. Grabbing a pad and pencil, ready to take down whatever message it might be for Frank, she hit the play button. Frank's voice greeted her, telling her that he would pick her up at one-thirty for a two o'clock appointment with Harry Wilton.

His voice sounded strained, distant, and Jane felt a curious sense of loss as she realized that in making love with him, in experiencing the intense intimacy they had shared, he'd shut his heart down.

She moved over to the window, absently scratching Mutt behind an ear as he nudged her in the back of the leg. If memory was a selective thing, then she'd do well to forget all about what she'd shared with Frank. Yet she had a feeling it was a memory that would haunt her for the rest of her life.

She rubbed her forehead tiredly. She felt as if she were being torn in two. If she wanted to continue a relationship with Frank, she needed to get her memories back. But she had a feeling those memories would reveal horrors that would make her insane.

Perhaps the best thing for her to do was leave here. Go to that women's shelter in Wilmington, forget she ever met a man named Frank Longford. Yes, perhaps that was what she should do...escape before her heart got so intricately involved with Frank's that she would be scarred forever. She swiped an errant tear that ran from her eye, then lightly touched the scar on the side of her neck. She didn't know what to do. She just didn't know what to do....

Frank pulled up in front of the house and looked at his wristwatch. One-thirty. Jane should be ready for her appointment with Harry. He got out of the car, a curious mix of dread and anticipation coursing through him as he walked toward the front door.

When he walked in, the first thing he saw was Jane's suitcase sitting in the foyer. The sight filled him with an unexpected sense of panic. "Jane?" he called out.

She came out of the living room, looking achingly lovely in her mint-green sundress. Over the course of the past week, she'd gotten some sun, and looked tanned and healthy. And more beautiful than ever. She walked over to stand next to the suitcase and looked at him hesitantly.

"I . . . uh . . . thought maybe you'd want me to go to that women's shelter in Wilmington." Her gaze didn't quite meet his. "I don't want to complicate your life, Frank."

"Don't be melodramatic," he snapped, pure panic making his tone more barbed than he intended. She looked up at him, her eyes wide, obviously startled by his sharpness. He couldn't imagine the house without her presence. He couldn't imagine coming home after a long day and not smelling the fragrance of her perfume, hearing the lilt of her voice as she greeted him.

"But, I thought maybe after last night—"

"Last night doesn't change anything." He raked a hand through his hair in distraction. "Jane, you don't have to leave. We're two rational adults. Last night was an error in judgment on both our parts, but nothing has to change. We can put it behind us and go on. We have to focus on what's important here, and the most important thing is your regaining your memory. Now, put your suitcase away."

Her eyes sparkled with tears of gratitude and he realized how much she had been dreading the shelter. She raised her arms, as if to give him a hug, then quickly dropped them to her side. "Thank you," she said huskily, then picked up the suitcase and took it into her bedroom.

Minutes later, they were on their way to Harry Wilton's office in downtown Garett Beach. "Nervous?"

he asked, noting the way she twisted the end of a strand of hair as she stared blankly out the window.

"A little," she admitted.

He turned his attention back to his driving. Every time he looked at her, his mind filled with visions of the way she had looked the night before, with her eyes glowing in passion and her body so soft and yielding beneath his. The images were positively mind-blowing.

He clenched his hands more tightly on the steering wheel, feeling the betrayal of his body as it responded to the thoughts in his head. Resisting, he focused on Gloria... all the lies she had told, all the plans he had made...plans he hadn't realized were built on her lies.

As he thought of Gloria's betrayal, his physical desire for Jane slowly cooled. He realized his past pain with Gloria was an effective tool to use against Jane. If he could remember the heartache he'd suffered with Gloria, he would maintain control and not allow himself to grow any closer to the woman beside him.

Still, it was with some relief that he wheeled into a parking space in front of Harry Wilton's office building. If there was going to be any hope of anything between himself and Jane, Harry was it. Within the next hour, it was possible Jane might remember everything about herself. She might discover, she was truly free to be with him.

"I'll just wait out here," he said as he took a seat in Harry's attractive waiting room.

She nodded, hesitating a moment, looking as if she wanted to say something. For a moment, her gaze lingered on him, touching him as intimately as any caress. Harry opened his inner-office door. He greeted her, and with a smile at Frank, he drew her inside his inner sanctum and closed the door.

Harry Wilton looked more like a gangster than a psychiatrist, Jane thought as she sat in the leather recliner chair across from where he sat behind his desk.

He was short and squat, with burly shoulders, the image of a gangster intensified by the unlit fat cigar he chewed and the massive gold ring that decorated one of his fingers. She could just imagine him playing a character in a bad B-rated movie, making somebody an offer they couldn't refuse. She swallowed the nervous giggle that sprang to her lips, realizing she was more than a little bit afraid of Dr. Wilton.

Was it possible that he could somehow dig into her brain and force her to look at the memories she feared? Despite her reluctance to know who she was, did he have some sort of magic that would override her reluctance and pull out her memories whether she wanted them or not?

Trepidation pulsed inside her as she stared at him, wondering what journey he might take her on, what visions from her past he might force her to relive.

"I think the best place to begin is for you to tell me about your earliest memory."

"That's easy. I woke up in the hospital and didn't know who or where I was."

From there, Dr. Wilton asked her about her other memories, the bits and pieces she'd recalled since awakening in the hospital. They talked about them, tried to dissect them, but nothing further revealed itself to Jane. He had her look at inkblots, play word-association games and make up stories to go with photographs, but none of it did a thing to advance her memory.

Jane told him of her fear of remembering, the fear that mingled with her desire to remember. She didn't tell him about her nightmares, about the horrible visions. She didn't tell him specifically what caused her fear, only that the thought of remembering worried her. He assured her that anxiety concerning remembering traumatic events was perfectly natural.

"Dr. Wilton, before we stop for the day, could I ask you a question?"

"Of course, my dear."

Jane felt the heat color her cheeks as she formulated the question she wanted to ask. "If before I got this amnesia I was married, or desperately in love with somebody... wouldn't I remember something of it? Wouldn't I know?"

Dr. Wilton smiled at her sympathetically. "It would be nice to think that our hearts remember what our minds forget, but unfortunately that isn't the case. Loved ones are wiped away in cases of amnesia as effectively as the trauma that caused the amnesia."

It was with a strange mixture of disappointment and relief that Jane left the office at the end of her hour. Frank stood up from his chair in the waiting room, his features momentarily showing an unguarded eagerness.

She shook her head, watching as he instantly schooled his face into a bland expression. "Nothing?" he asked as she approached him.

"Nothing."

"Well, we can't expect miracles out of one therapy session."

They were both silent as they got into the car and headed home. Frank's disappointment evoked a deep guilt within her. She knew she hadn't tried hard enough with Dr. Wilton. But she was afraid, so very afraid of what secrets were contained in her head.

She'd answered all his questions, but she hadn't attempted to brush away the gray cobwebs that obscured her mind. And now she couldn't even offer Frank the assurance that she hadn't been in love, didn't have anyone to return to, wouldn't leave him to run to another man's arms.

A headache blossomed in the center of her forehead, and she worried at it with the tips of her fingers. She was so confused. It was a case of damned if she did, damned if she didn't. If she didn't ever remember her past, then Frank had made it clear that there would be no relationship between them. But what good would it do for her to remember and him to realize she was a horrible person who'd done terrible things... a person he *couldn't* have a relationship with? *Damned if she did, damned if she didn't.* She ended up the loser no matter what she did.

She leaned her head against the window and closed her eyes. She shoved all thoughts out of her mind, letting the motion of the car lull her into numbness.

A picture began to unfold in her mind. A baby boy wrapped in a blue blanket with rocking horses dancing across lace. She felt the weight of the baby in her arms, smelled the sweetness that emanated from the tiny bundle.

She was rocking the baby, jiggling him, crooning to him in an attempt to stop his fussiness. "Shh, you're disturbing everyone," she whispered, holding him against her heart. She walked with him, pacing a small confined area, trying to still his shrill squeals of displeasure.

"Can't you shut that kid up?" a voice bellowed from somewhere nearby.

"I'm doing the best I can," she replied tightly. Eyes glared at her and the child.

The scene changed, shifted, melted into flames of fire, the scent of kerosene and death. No...she reached to reclaim the memory of the baby, the sweetness of the bundle in her arms, but it was no longer there. Fire usurped her brain...fire and death.

She snapped her eyes open with a gasp, not wanting to see anymore. Her heart thudded loudly and she looked over at Frank to see if he could hear her terror. His attention was focused on the road, or somewhere on his own thoughts. He didn't seem aware of her at all.

She stared out the window, but didn't pay attention to the scenery flashing by, her brain racing with questions and suppositions.

Who was the child? Was it hers? A pain centered itself in her heart at the thought. What had happened to the child? Who was the man in her vision? A husband? A lover? Where was he?

And yet, even as she asked herself these questions, the horrifying answers were there. They were dead. The baby was dead. The man was dead. They had burned in a fire. And each time she saw those visions of the fire, smelled the kerosene-like odor, she felt an overwhelming guilt.

I did it. She jammed a knuckle against her mouth to still the cry of anguish. Somehow, she had torched and killed people. She was responsible for their deaths. She was guilty... *guilty*.

But I'm not a bad person, her mind screamed rebelliously. How do you know you aren't? a tiny voice niggled deep inside. You don't know who you are or what you're capable of. You don't know what kind of evil may be in your heart. *But not murder,* her heart cried.

And yet, all her memories, all the visions, all the evidence, pointed to the fact that she was guilty. When she'd checked into that beachfront cottage, she'd apparently been running away, using an assumed name. She'd changed her appearance. She'd done everything that a criminal would do. *She'd done everything a guilty person would do.*

Had she had a baby and a husband, and through stress or some sort of psychotic breakdown, committed arson and murder? Had she waited until the dark hours of night, then poured kerosene and lit a match? She didn't want to know. She positively did not want to know. She had a feeling if she knew the truth, she would lose her mind. She wouldn't be able to live with the reality of what she'd done.

She looked over at Frank, once again jamming her knuckles against her mouth to stifle her cry of despair. He was a good man, a man with character and heart.

She turned and stared out the window again. She wondered what he would do if he realized he'd made love to a woman who might possibly have committed murder?

Chapter 10

Frank sat on the sofa, trying to concentrate on the book opened on his lap, but his attention kept straying to where Jane lay on the floor playing with the dogs.

She had a knotted sock and was playing tug-of-war with first one, then the other. Occasionally, her musical laughter would ring out and his stomach muscles would clench against the evocative sound.

It had been two weeks since they had shared their night of passion, two weeks of sharing space with her and trying to ignore the taunting desire that tempted him every moment of every day.

She'd been to see Harry twice, but with little result. Odd memories had surfaced, but nothing that brought them any closer to knowing who she was or where she had come from.

Maybe she's an alien, he thought with a touch of irritation. Yes, that was it. She'd been dropped from a spaceship to wreak havoc on his libido. She was definitely succeeding at her assigned task, he thought wryly.

If anything, it was worse now that he knew what it was like to make love with her. He didn't have to fantasize how her long legs would feel locked around him...he knew. He didn't have to imagine the taste of her soft, sweet lips...he knew. And his knowledge only increased the sharp ache in the pit of his stomach.

He shifted position on the sofa so she wasn't in his direct line of vision. He refocused his gaze on the book he wasn't reading, staring blankly at the pages.

He stiffened again as she giggled and growled at the dogs, playfully wrestling with Jeff as Mutt ran around her and gave sharp yips of excitement.

"Mutt, knock it off," he yelled, his control on his irritation abruptly snapping. The dog immediately sat down and stared at Frank in confusion.

Jane sat up and placed an arm around the errant dog. "Please don't yell at him. It wasn't his fault. I'm the one who got him all excited and I apologize."

His anger dissipated immediately. How could he remain angry when her eyes sparkled so beguilingly, when the touch of an impudent smile lingered at one corner of her mouth? It was impossible to stay angry. "It's all right," he replied gruffly.

He stood up and slapped the book down on the table. He paced the room, trying to work off the tension that coiled inside him like a tightly wound spring. "I'm just restless," he muttered. The air in the house seemed to crackle with the electricity that zapped his insides. He stopped and looked at her. "How would you like to go to a movie?" he asked suddenly.

"A movie?" She got up off the floor and looked at him curiously. "Well, sure . . . if you want to."

Hell, no, he didn't want to go to the movies. What he wanted to do was take her into his bedroom and make love until the sun came up. What he wanted to do was trail hungry kisses down the length of her body until she whimpered and screamed in passionate release. But he couldn't do that, and he also knew if he had to spend one more minute alone with her in this house, he would go mad.

"Yes, I want to," he replied tersely. He looked at his wristwatch. "If we leave here in the next fifteen minutes or so, we should be able to make the seven-thirty show."

"I'll just go change," she said, and disappeared in the direction of her bedroom.

He breathed a sigh of relief as she left the room. Surely in the crowded confines of a movie theater, surrounded by a crowd of other people, he could regain some control over himself and his raging desire. Surely he could lose himself in whatever story unfolded on the big screen and not obsess on Jane.

Obsess on Jane . . . That was exactly what he had been doing in the past two weeks. She filled his every moment. Teasing images haunted his every waking hour, and each night she visited him in his dreams, leaving him to awaken feeling needy and bereft.

Before he had obsessed on work, on filling each hour of every day so he would return home to the silence only when exhausted enough to fall into bed. Now he found himself leaving the hospital the moment his job was finished. He wasn't volunteering the same amount of hours at the clinic or at the nursing home. He no longer took evening appointments at his office. She was making changes in his life and he wasn't sure if they were good or bad. He only knew they frightened him.

"All ready," she said from behind him.

He turned around and the sight of her made his heart ache. Why couldn't he have found an ugly duckling lying unconscious on his beach? Why did she have to be a swan? He'd never seen her look so lovely. She wore a dress he hadn't seen before, a simple peach-colored one with short puffy sleeves and a cinched waist that emphasized her slenderness.

She looked like a juicy, ripe peach, ready to be plucked and enjoyed. It was only when he looked deep in her eyes that he saw the peach was bruised within. Dark shadows, internal pain, deep secrets lingered there . . . secrets that made Frank wary, afraid to enjoy the sum of her sweetness.

"Frank?" She looked at him questioningly, and he flushed, realizing he'd been staring.

"New dress?"

She nodded. "Some of the volunteers went shopping last week on our lunch hour. Thanks to your generous salary, I'm slowly adding to my meager wardrobe."

"It looks nice," he said, studiously ignoring the way her eyes flared with pleasure at his compliment. "And if we're going to make that show, we'd better get going."

"I keep hearing good things about your volunteer work at the hospital," he said a few minutes later as they drove toward town.

"I'm really enjoying my time there. There's something very satisfying about helping people." She looked at him and smiled. "You must get an enormous sense of satisfaction out of being a doctor."

"I do." But not as much as I used to, he wanted to add. And it was true. Before Jane, his work had always filled him with an enormous sense of satisfaction. But lately, it wasn't enough. Despite the fact that he had long ago decided to live a solitary life, he was beginning to recognize the loneliness in having chosen that particular path.

"Everyone has been talking about the Fourth of July celebration next week," Jane said.

"Garett Beach goes a little crazy on the fourth," Frank replied. "There's a parade in the morning, then a big barbecue throughout the day, then, of course, the required fireworks display that night. The chamber of commerce goes all out to make it a full day of fun."

"Sounds marvelous," she said enthusiastically.

"I'm off that day. We could go if you want to."

"Oh, I'd love to," she agreed instantly.

They fell into silence, the car's air-conditioning providing relief from the outside heat and humidity. Frank wished he could roll down the windows and breathe in the scent of the ocean instead of the whispering scent of her seductive perfume. But he knew the heat would quickly wear on them, and it was ridiculous to suffer just for the sake of not breathing in the essence of Jane.

It was with enormous relief that he pulled into the theater parking lot, pleased to see it nearly full. Good, there would be plenty of other people in the theater. The scent of other people, buttery popcorn, grilling hot dogs would be strong enough that he wouldn't be able to smell the sensual floral scent of her.

"Uh-oh," Jane said with a laugh as they walked around to the front of the theater.

"What?" Frank looked at her curiously.

She pointed up to the marquee. "Tonight is monster night at the movies. *The Monster From the Deep, Outer Space Aliens....* It looks like we're in for a treat."

"You still want to go?" Frank asked dubiously.

"Why not?" she replied with a bright smile. "We're already here and it might be a lot of fun." She linked her arm through his in a completely unconscious gesture of familiarity. "Besides, I remember the first time I saw *The Thing*. It was a delicious kind of shivery fun to be vicariously scared to death." The minute the words left her mouth, she stopped and stared at him, then shook her head wryly. "Another inane memory to add to the growing list."

He squeezed her arm, recognizing her frustration. "But at least you're still remembering things. Medically that's a very good sign. Eventually, you will remember, Jane. You'll remember it all."

She nodded solemnly. She remained quiet, withdrawn, as he bought their tickets and they found a seat in the crowded theater. He found himself wondering what she was thinking about, wishing he could crawl into her head and share all her thoughts, all her dreams.

He forced his attention to the theater full of people. He'd decided to come here in an effort to stop thinking about her, stop wanting her. He nodded and waved at various patients he saw, smiling as he saw Cindy approach them.

"Hi, Dr. Longford," she greeted, her gaze openly curious as it lingered on Jane. "I didn't know you liked the movies."

"Only monster movies," Frank replied with a warm smile. "Cindy, this is Jane, a friend of mine." He looked at Jane. "Cindy is a former patient of mine. Her mother works at the hospital."

"Oh, do I know her?" Jane asked.

Frank shook his head. "I doubt it, she works the night shift."

For a few minutes, Jane and Cindy visited, talking about the upcoming movie and Cindy's summer fun, then Cindy excused herself and went back to her friends who sat in a row at the front of the theater.

"She's a cute kid," Jane observed when the teenager was gone.

"She likes you," Frank observed. "Normally, she's quite shy with adults."

Jane smiled. "At least she didn't ask me what it's like to not know who I am. Thank goodness the novelty of my amnesia is slowly wearing off on the good people of Garett Beach. Most of them just see me as Jane Smith, hospital volunteer and housekeeper to Doc Longford."

Then, the lights dimmed and the previews of upcoming movies began to play on the screen. Frank made a fast trip to the concession stand, buying a tub of buttered popcorn and two soft drinks.

As he settled back next to Jane, he tried to concentrate on the screen. He could still smell her...that faint floral scent that so enticed his senses. The theater smells didn't overwhelm her subtle scent, as he'd hoped.

As the movie began, she seemed to relax against him, her warm shoulder against his, filling his body with a fevered heat. If the popcorn on his knee had been a container full of kernels, he knew they would have exploded as a result of the heat filling him.

He reached for a handful of the buttery treat, her hand moving to do the same. "Sorry," she whispered with a smile as their hands bumped together.

He nodded stiffly, wishing the theater seats were bigger, with more space in between. He'd come here to escape the very desire that now swept through him.

His desire for her was slowly torturing him into madness.

Jane was intensely aware of the tension in Frank. He leaned away from her, a muscle in his jaw knotting and unknotting, and she knew it was the same kind of tension that had been her constant companion since the night they had made love.

She wished things could be different. She wished he would throw his arm around her shoulders, cuddle her against him, whisper in her ear of the passion they'd share when the movie was over and they were back home.

She wished he could just be satisfied with who she was now, what she was doing with her life at this moment. She'd steadfastly refused to delve into her past over the last two weeks.

She'd come to the decision that her past was gone. She didn't know what she had done, whom she might have hurt, but the person who'd possibly done the horrible things she dreamed of had nothing to do with the person she was now.

She was building a life here in Garett Beach, a life she was proud of, and she didn't want to go back and claim the evil she feared blackened her past.

More than anything, she wanted Frank to make love to her again. In the single act of lovemaking they'd shared, he'd made her realize that she was a passionate woman, loved the act of making love and communicating tender emotions without words. She longed to feel his touch, his heated caresses, wanted his overwhelming passion to surround her, keep her safe forever.

She sighed and refocused on the movie, where an alien with a laser gun was terrorizing a roomful of people. She wished she could change Frank's mind about needing to know her past. She wished Jane Smith could be enough for him.

It was nearly three hours later when the second movie ended and they moved into the aisle to exit the theater. Jane stood just behind Frank, feeling the press of eager bodies behind her.

A wave of discomfort flooded through her as an inexplicable panic crawled up her throat.

Bodies shoving, straining, fighting to get out. Screams of terror, of pain... She closed her eyes against the flashes of visions that removed her from the movie theater and placed her in the middle of one of her nightmares.

Darkness all around. Her heart raced painfully in her chest and a cold perspiration broke out across her forehead. Out...she had to get out. She smelled smoke...fire. She was going to be ill. She was going to scream.

Just as she was about to release the scream trapped deep within her, she found herself standing out on the sidewalk in front of the theater, gulping the oppressive air as if it were pure oxygen.

"Are you all right?"

She stared at him, noting the worried lines that creased his forehead. She nodded, waiting for normalcy to return, for her pulse to slow and the sick sensation to pass. "Yes," she said faintly, taking another deep breath. "Yes, I just got a little claustrophobic for a moment."

"Why don't we go over to the café and get a piece of pie before we head back?" Frank suggested.

"Okay," she agreed, wondering if sweets could take the place of sex or cure strange, frightening hallucinations.

By the time they'd walked across the street and down the block to the café, Jane was feeling better. Although she was aware that the outing had done nothing to alleviate the strain between them.

She felt as though every one of her nerve endings were frayed, and a restless energy caused her to feel like jumping out of her skin. She knew Frank was stalling the moment when they would return to the house and once again be completely alone.

There were only two other couples in the café when they entered and walked toward a booth in the back. As they settled in across from each other, the waitress approached. They placed their order and while they waited for her to return with their pie and coffee, Jane looked over at the couple sitting nearby.

They were young and obviously in love. Before each of them was a dish of ice cream, now melted into soup, but neither seemed in a hurry to eat. They held hands across the table, staring into each other's eyes, murmuring in low lover-tones.

A deep ache pierced Jane's heart as she watched, envying them their lover's talk, their intimate preoccupation with each other. She wanted that for herself. She wanted it for Frank. It was the kind of connection, the sort of special commitment that blossomed when hearts touched and souls entwined.

She looked at Frank, vaguely surprised to see him also staring at the couple. As if he sensed her gaze on him, he turned and looked at her, and in his eyes she saw the same hunger, the same need that burned within her. It was there for only a single second, then gone, as if a protective shield had snapped firmly into place. He quickly picked up his fork and scrutinized it.

Again Jane felt a sweeping despair as she realized the man she wanted that kind of relationship with wasn't willing to have one with her. And the one thing Frank demanded of her, a plunge into the hellish nightmares of her past, she wasn't willing to give. She was afraid that by doing that, the only thing she would accomplish would be to show him she was a horrible person, one he couldn't possibly love. They were at an impasse, and she had a feeling no matter which way they turned, they would both be losers.

She sighed as the waitress arrived at their table with their orders. "Ah, there's nothing better to satisfy the soul than a hunk of warm apple pie," Frank exclaimed as the waitress left.

Jane nodded, but she could think of something to indulge in that was much more soul-satisfying than a piece of pastry. "Tell me more about this Fourth of July celebration," she urged, needing pleasant conversation to alleviate some of the palpable strain between them.

"Last year, I got all my impressions of the celebration from the inside of the emergency room. Most of what I treated was overindulgence—stomachaches from overeating, intoxication from overimbibing, parents allowing their kids to play with firecrackers. Several people came in with sprained ankles and pulled muscles, their trophies from the sack- and three-legged races. This year I have the day off, so I'll be among the revelers, instead of treating the revelers."

"And do you plan to overindulge?" Jane asked teasingly.

He grinned. "I might eat a little too much, but I don't drink and I definitely won't be involved in the races."

"So you're more of an observer than an active participant."

"I guess so."

Jane watched indulgently as he finished his pie and signaled the waitress for another slice. He grinned sheepishly. "I told you I had a weakness for pie."

For the next few minutes, they talked about the town, about the upcoming celebration, about the hospital. Slowly, almost imperceptibly, the tension began to ease, replaced by the warmth and familiarity that marked their relationship.

It wasn't until they were back in the car, heading toward home, that the tension reappeared, like an unwelcome guest who refused to go away.

"It looks like we're in for a storm," he observed, reaching over and turning on the car radio.

As mellow music filled the interior of the car, Jane looked out the window, observing that the stars were obscured with a thick layer of clouds. Yes, there was definitely a storm brewing out there. But there was also one building up inside her, one that could challenge nature's in its fury and power.

She stirred restlessly, fighting the impulse to reach over and place her hand on the taut muscles of his thigh. Instead, she leaned her head back and closed her eyes, trying to ease her own inner pressure. Pressure...yes, she felt like a pressure cooker about to blow its top, and she knew the only thing that could ease it was Frank. She needed his arms around her. She needed to feel his body moving against hers, filling her up. She wanted his mouth on hers, his tongue tasting of hot desire. A small groan escaped her lips.

"Something wrong?" Frank asked.

"Uh...no." She sat up straight and opened her eyes. "Just a little indigestion," she fabricated. "Probably too much pie on top of all that popcorn."

She looked over at him, noted the way he gripped the steering wheel so tightly his knuckles were white. Obviously he was suffering the same sort of "indigestion."

By the time they reached the house, the air between them was as oppressive and heavy as the air outside. He slammed his car door with more force than necessary, his entire body rigid as he unlocked the front door and they entered.

Mutt and Jeff greeted them enthusiastically and Frank let them out the back door. "I think I'll change clothes and go for a quick run on the beach." Without waiting for her reply, he went to his bedroom.

Jane moved over to the sliding glass door and stared out into the darkness. She could just make out the silhouettes of the two dogs running along the edge of the water. That was what she needed to do—run with the wind whipping at her hair, run out all the useless energy that tingled inside her. She knew that was what Frank intended to do.

She turned around as he came back into the room, a sleeveless sweatshirt and jogging shorts displaying his body's perfection. He strode to the door and whistled for the dogs. "I don't want them nipping at my heels," he explained, not looking at her.

The dogs came back in and he stepped out onto the deck. "I'll be back later," he said, then disappeared into the heat and humidity of the night.

Jane gave the dogs water, then closed them in the kitchen area, where they spent their nights. She then went into her bedroom and undressed. Her body ached with need, her heart heavy.

It didn't seem fair. It was obvious Frank wanted her as much as she wanted him, yet they denied themselves the very thing they both craved. It was crazy.

She pulled her nightgown over her head, running her hands down the smooth silk. It was a new gown, much like the one she'd been wearing on the night Frank had found her on the beach. Fitted to the waist, it billowed in folds to the floor. Wearing it made her feel beautiful, tempting and desirable.

"A lot of good it does me," she thought irritably, knowing she was wound too tight to go immediately to bed. She paced the floor for a few minutes, the tension not easing, but building to volcanic proportions.

She'd bought the nightgown at the same time she'd bought the dress she'd worn earlier, at the same time she'd bought a bottle of dye to retouch the roots of her hair. When she'd picked up the gown, she'd immediately envisioned wearing it for Frank, knowing he'd be pleased by the sensual silk, the romantic cut of the garment.

She drifted back out to the living room, back to the sliding glass door. She leaned her head against the glass and stared outside, looking for Frank on the dark beach. In the distance, lightning illuminated the clouds, portending the coming storm.

She spotted him jogging in the distance, a solitary silhouette against the ocean waves. He looked so isolated, so lonely, and her heart echoed with the same sense of isolation and loneliness.

"This is crazy," she muttered to herself. They were both rational adults. They wanted each other. So why was he out there running like a crazy fool and she was in here, longing for his touch?

She slid open the door and stepped outside on the wooden deck. Immediately the heavy air surrounded her and the wind lifted her hair with sultry fingers.

She leaned her head back and closed her eyes, an internal battle waging between good sense and passion. The wind whipped her skirt around her legs, and all her senses seemed intensely acute. She could smell the water, the sand and the faint sulfuric scent of the storm's approach. She could hear the wind chimes ringing discordantly in the gusts of air that preceded the coming squall. She felt achingly alive and knew exactly what she wanted to do.

She made her decision and stepped off the deck and onto the warmth of the sand. Eyes squinted, looking for Frank, she walked with determined steps, knowing she was about to brave the storm.

Chapter 11

Frank ran as if trying to outrace the wind. But it wasn't the wind he was attempting to outdistance...it was desire. It surged inside his veins with an all-consuming power. It raged in his head like a monster out of control.

Jane...Jane...his heart pounded the rhythm of her name. No, not her name, he corrected himself. But her name didn't matter. She was merely the woman he desired more than he could ever remember desiring anyone else.

He stopped his frantic pace, knowing it was an exercise in futility. He knew he couldn't outrun his desire. He'd have to run forever to even begin to do that.

He leaned forward and braced his hands against his knees, letting the refreshing wind off the water cool him down as he took deep, cleansing breaths. He straightened, his gaze captured by the lightning flashing in the distance. A moment or two later, thunder rumbled like angry gods voicing extreme displeasure. He raked his hands through his hair, then turned around to head back to the house.

He'd walked only a few yards when he saw her. At first, he thought she was a figment of his imagination, a vision conjured up by his intense need.

She seemed to float on the wind, her pale nightgown luminous in the surrounding darkness as it billowed on the breeze. Her dark hair whipped around her head, dancing tendrils that taunted and teased.

His blood surged through him, filling his veins with overpowering emotion, making his heart pound in an unsteady beat. She was once again his mystery lady, the one who'd so captured his imagination as night after night he'd watched her walk the beach alone.

But she was no longer a complete mystery. Now he knew the taste of her skin, knew the warmth that waited there to pull him into splendor, knew the heavenly sound of her cries against his neck as he enveloped himself in her heat.

He stopped walking, merely watching as she advanced toward him. He knew why she had come to him, knew that he was powerless to fight against the forces of passion that pulsated in the air.

She stopped inches from where he stood motionless. He could smell her feminine, floral scent mingling with the salty smell of the ocean and the slightly sulfuric tang of the storm. Her eyes glowed with almost iridescent flecks, holding a question...a plea...a demand he couldn't ignore.

With a harsh groan, he pulled her to him, devouring her mouth with a white-hot lightning to rival the electricity in the distant sky. She returned his kiss, searing his mouth with an electric surge of her own.

She wrapped her arms around him, arching her body into his, meeting his strength, his need, with a yielding softness that made him groan once again. He cupped her buttocks, pulling her closer against him, letting her know the full extent of his arousal.

God, how he loved the feel of her. How he loved the scent of her. He didn't want to think anymore. He only wanted to feel, to be...to love.

As if in unspoken communication, they both went to their knees in the sand, their mouths still touching as their hands caressed feverishly.

Jane felt as if she'd stepped into a dream. The hot breeze was like a thousand fingers dancing up and down her flesh, but it was Frank's fingertips that burned into her heart, smoked in her soul.

She dropped her head back, shivering as his lips danced across her jawline, down her neck, lingering at the deep vee of her gown. As the tip of his tongue licked along the material, Jane's breath caught in her throat.

In one fluid movement, she swept the gown up over her head and placed it on the sand. Then she lay down on it, motioning him into her arms.

He didn't hesitate. He quickly removed his clothes and covered her nakedness with his own. The tension that had filled Jane for the past two weeks escaped her in a sigh as she felt his smooth, warm flesh against her own.

Yes, this was where she belonged. This was where she was meant to spend eternity. She wanted Frank next to her for today and always. She needed him to make her whole.

And then she couldn't think anymore. She could only feel. His hands moved in reverent caresses, stroking from her neck to the fullness of her breasts. They lingered there only a moment, then continued their trail of fire, down her rib cage, across her hips, down the lower portion of her abdomen to the place where she needed his touch most of all.

She arched up to meet him, crying his name into the wind as the heat inside her exploded, leaving her quivering and breathless beneath him. Still he didn't stop. He continued to work his magic until once again the tension inside her built and she clawed at his back, letting him know she needed him to complete what he had begun.

He took her without hesitation, plunging into her depths as he moaned her name. Jane shuddered as he pulled her into the vortex of a storm so intense it possessed her, consumed her.

He became the raging winds, the sultry night, the very storm itself as he moved inside her with a fierceness meant to complete his possession of her. As his maleness filled her so completely, his mouth completed the intimate connection by covering hers with a scorching heat that brought tears of pleasure to her eyes.

As she felt him swell inside her, stiffening in release, she felt her own crescendo rushing through her and stealing her breath.

For several long moments, they remained entwined, Frank bracing the bulk of his weight with his elbows. She wondered vaguely if the deep rumble she heard was the clouds clapping together overhead or the thunderous rhythm of their hearts beating in unison. She tried to will the storm away, wanting to remain here in his arms forever. But as lightning once again danced across the heavens followed by an instant crash of thunder, he moved to get up.

As he lifted himself away from her, a drop of moisture fell onto her cheek. At first she thought it was a drop of rain, but in the moment before he grabbed his clothes and turned away, she saw the shimmer of tears that garnished his strong features.

"Frank?" She watched as he pulled his shorts on, then swiped at his face before he turned to look at her. His features were hardened, distant, and she shivered, unsure if the shiver came from the coldness of his eyes or the sudden chilliness of the surrounding air. "Please talk to me. Tell me what you're thinking, what's going on in your mind," she said softly.

She reached for her nightgown, gave it a cursory shake to remove the sand from it, then pulled it over her head. She looked at him expectantly, watching as nearby lightning split the night and illuminated his features in stark brilliance. "Please, Frank. Talk to me," she repeated. At that moment, thunder boomed directly overhead and huge raindrops splattered down.

"We'd better get inside," he said. He grabbed her hand and pulled her up, then together they ran for the safety of the house.

Once inside, Jane quickly showered and changed clothes, then Frank did the same. "Okay, we'll talk," he finally said as they sat in the living room and the storm knocked loudly on the windows. He got up from the sofa and began to pace the floor, his hand splaying through his damp dark hair.

"Jane, I can't continue this way." He stopped his pacing and looked at her, vulnerability shining from his dark eyes. "I care about you very much, and each time we make love, I care a little more deeply. But I can't keep getting in deeper and deeper with you. It's not right, it's foolishness of the worst kind."

"Why? Why can't we just pretend I was born on the beach where you found me, that my life began at that moment?" Jane stood up, needing to persuade him, wanting him to accept her without any baggage from the past. "I *like* Jane Smith. I'm working hard to make a good life here. Why can't I just be Jane Smith for the rest of my life?"

"Because you aren't Jane Smith," he returned, a vein throbbing in the side of his neck. "And no amount of pretending is going to make you who you aren't."

He reached out and grabbed her shoulders, his fingers biting painfully into her tender flesh as his features twisted with torment. "I can't live a life with you, constantly looking over my shoulder, wondering when somebody from your past will reach out and reclaim you, pull you back where you truly belong.''

He released her and stepped back, some of his fervency dissipating. "I thought the past didn't matter once before." His voice was low and unsteady. "I was told it was unimportant, that what was important was where we were going...not where we'd been."

"With Gloria?" Jane asked.

He looked at her in surprise. "How do you know about her?"

"I don't know much. Only that she was a tourist and you planned to marry her, then she left and never came back."

He shook his head. "I should have known somebody would mention her to you, that nothing remains a secret for very long in Garett Beach." He sat down on the sofa and buried his face in his hands, his shoulders slumped forward in a gesture of defeat that tore at her heart.

She fought the need to go to him, put her arms around him and comfort him, knowing instinctively he would rebuff her efforts.

He took a deep breath and looked at her once again, his eyes deep and fathomless. "Gloria came here on vacation and we immediately hit it off. It was a whirlwind kind of thing, intense and crazy. I kept asking her about her family, her past, but she told me none of that was important, that as far as she was concerned she'd begun life when she'd come to Garett Beach and fallen in love with me. At that time, it was a heady, powerful feeling and it only made me fall more deeply in love with her.''

He broke off and his gaze was unfocused. He frowned thoughtfully. "I allowed myself to fall into a sort of fool's paradise with Gloria. I decided she was right, it didn't matter what her life had been before she came to Garett Beach. All that mattered was that we were together and we were in love.''

"And so you planned your wedding?" Jane asked, knowing that much from what she'd heard through the gossip mill.

He nodded. "We reserved the church, ordered the flowers, bought the rings. Then, on the morning of the wedding, I received a note and in it she told me that she had three kids and a husband waiting for her to come home.''

Jane hissed in a swift intake of breath, her heart aching in sympathy for the betrayal he'd suffered. "Oh, Frank," she whispered.

He smiled, an oddly bewildered, achingly vulnerable smile. "It seems Gloria was suffering from depression. Her husband thought some time away from him and the kids would help her.''

"Yes, but she lied to you.''

"A lie of omission. I can't really blame her. I was as much at fault as she was. She got as caught up in the moment as I did. I allowed her to convince me that her past didn't matter because I didn't want to know there might be anything that would dispel the magic.''

His eyes closed as if against a wave of pain. "Jane... I can't do it again. I can't go through the same kind of hurt. I won't ignore the strength of the past, its power to reclaim love with memories of others, the power to taint the future with unfinished business. I can't do it again, Jane. I refuse to fall in love with a woman who has no past."

"But that's not fair," Jane protested, a tightness in her chest squeezing her heart. "You're punishing me for Gloria's mistakes. She refused to tell you about her past. I *can't* tell you about mine."

Frank smiled sadly. "But the result is the same."

"But I'm not Gloria and I can't give you what I don't possess, and I don't possess my memories." Swift anger swept through her, anger not only at him, but at the fates that had placed her in this position. "You aren't being fair," she exclaimed.

He stood up, regret darkening the liquid depths of his eyes. "Fair doesn't play into this." He drew a deep breath. "There will be no more lapses of control... no more lovemaking between us. Until you regain possession of your memory, we'll conduct ourselves as friends, but we won't be lovers again."

Jane smiled with a touch of bitterness. "How ironic that it's your past interfering in our present."

He shrugged helplessly. "The past and the present are intrinsically intertwined, we can't escape from either." He didn't wait for an answer, but turned and went to his bedroom, closing the door with a finality that echoed in the chambers of Jane's heart.

A fool's paradise...wasn't that what Frank had said he and Gloria had been living? And wasn't that what she herself had been living in? The nightmares, the horrifying visions, the overwhelming guilt that plagued her with each horrid piece of that particular memory. How could she think it was all powerless to affect her?

She moved to stand at the sliding door, watching nature vent its energy. Only moments before, the beach had been witness to their lovemaking. Now it was suffering the effects of nature's tumultuous disposition. The remnants of their union, the impressions of their bodies in the sand, would no longer be there in the morning. But the memory of what they had shared would always be a souvenir she'd carry deep within her brain, deep within her heart.

She knew Frank meant what he'd said. He wouldn't touch her again until he knew for sure that she was free from any claims from her past. She'd seen the determined thrust of his jaw, the resolution in his eyes as he'd made the statement. He wouldn't allow passion to overwhelm good sense again.

Jane closed her eyes, hot tears burning them. She knew she had a choice. If she didn't retrieve her past, there would never be a chance for her and Frank to build something good, something substantial together.

"Oh God, what do I do? What do I do?" she moaned, fisting her hands and placing them on either side of her head. She should leave, get out of here before she hurt Frank more deeply. Before she herself was scarred even more deeply.

She reached up and touched the scar on her neck. She should escape before her memories fully returned, before she saw the tenderness in Frank's eyes transform to horror. She should leave before he discovered what a horrible person she was . . . what horrible things she might have done.

But where would she go? How would she live? How could she live with herself knowing the evil things she might have done? More important, she realized she didn't want to go. She didn't want to leave Frank. Not ever.

"Jane?"

She whirled around at the sound of his voice, tears blurring her vision as she stared at him. He suddenly looked haggard, as if in the past few minutes since leaving her, he'd fought an enormous battle that had tremendously wearied him.

"I lied." His voice trembled with suppressed emotion. "I want you again . . . even now. There's no way I'll be able to live with you every day and not want you again and again." He heaved a weighty sigh. "I'm not strong enough to stay away from you by willpower alone."

"Do you want me to leave?" she asked faintly, trembling at the thought of going away, never seeing him again.

"No." The single word exploded from him as if propelled by an undeniable force. "No," he repeated more softly. "I want you to stay, and I want to make love to you again. I guess we'll just have to face the uncertainty of your future when you finally remember your past."

For a moment, Jane stared at him, her eyes once again veiling with tears as she realized the sacrifice he was making. He cared about her enough to gamble, to risk heartache.

She knew it was now up to her. She had a decision to make. God help her, she was falling in love with Frank, and the thought both exhilarated and frightened her.

She had to gamble, had to hope that in recovering her memories she wouldn't destroy what they had between them. She could only hope that he would care so deeply about her that it wouldn't matter what she had done in the past.

He held out his arms and she went to him, leaning her head against the strength and warmth of his broad chest. She buried her head against him, as always feeling warm and protected when in his arms.

She knew now she had to actively work to regain her memories. She had to remember what she'd done, then decide if she could share that past with Frank. She didn't want to remember, but she would do it for Frank. She just hoped that in doing so, she didn't destroy them both.

She began her search for her memory in the library, scanning newspapers for any story of arson and murder that might jog her memory. She looked at all the papers from nearby towns, knowing whatever it was would appear as a news article within the last six months. She'd asked Frank about the scar tissue on her neck, and he'd guessed the scar to be about four to six months old. She knew the burn that had created the scar had occurred at the same time of the fire that haunted her.

It felt strange, to be actively seeking answers to the puzzle she'd tried for so long to shove away. Even though every night she slept in Frank's arms, awakened beside him each morning, despite the fact that she knew he cared about her, desired her, she was aware that he held back a small piece of himself.

She couldn't blame him, knew it was a form of self-protection. She, too, held back. She hadn't shared with him her visions, didn't want to until she knew for sure exactly what they meant. Although she knew Frank cared about her, and she cared deeply about him, there was a lack of trust that couldn't be bridged until she shared with him all she feared.

He seemed to sense that she was holding back. Although he didn't say a word, it only made Jane feel worse. But it was this that created a chasm between them, one barely perceptible, but there nevertheless.

She now refocused her attention on the newspapers before her, thumbing through the pages with a sense of futility. Death and destruction were on every page—murder and mayhem in black and white, but nothing about an arson-murder involving the death of an infant and a man. Nothing that niggled any corner of Jane's mind with familiarity.

She looked at her watch and sighed. It was almost time for Etta to pick her up. On the days that Jane didn't volunteer at the hospital, Frank had dropped her off at the library and Etta had picked her up to

take her back home. Both Frank and Etta knew Jane
was hunting for something that would jog her memory, but neither of them knew it was the report of a
murder that she sought.

She returned her stack of newspapers to the woman
at the desk, then went out the front door and leaned
against the building as she watched for Etta's car.

She smiled faintly as she saw the red, white and blue
streamers that decorated the streets. The town was
poised for the big celebration to take place on the next
day and a ripple of pleasant anticipation danced inside her as she thought of sharing that day with Frank.

Tomorrow I won't even think about this mess, she
told herself sternly. Just for tomorrow she would allow herself to enjoy being Jane Smith, a resident of
Garett Beach. She wouldn't allow any visions, any
terrible flashes in her mind to taint the celebration of
the country's independence.

She frowned as she noticed a man sitting in a parked
blue car on the other side of the street. Strange, she
could have sworn he had been there when she'd gone
into the library several hours before. She felt his gaze
on her, a steady scrutiny that made an anxious unease
unfurl in her stomach.

She looked away, down the street in the direction
from which Etta would come. When she looked back
at the man in the car, his gaze was still steady on her.

She sighed in relief as Etta pulled up in front of her.
She scrambled into the car, turning to cast a backward glance at the strange man as they drove off.

"Find anything interesting today?" Etta asked.

Jane shook her head. "Nothing. I've looked at maps, studied the names of cities and towns all over the East Coast, and nothing feels right."

Etta reached over and patted Jane's hand in her usual maternal fashion. "Don't force it. Eventually it will all break open and you'll know more about yourself than you ever wanted to know." Etta chuckled. "There are a few incidents in my checkered past I'd just as soon forget forever."

Jane forced a smile to her lips, casting a glance over her shoulder to see if the man in the blue car was anywhere in sight. She breathed a sigh of relief when she didn't see him.

"What's the matter with you? You're as jumpy as feet on hot sand."

"Oh . . . nothing. There was just a strange man outside the library. He was staring at me." She fought off a shiver of apprehension.

Etta laughed. "Honey, if I looked as good as you, strange men would stare at me, too!"

Was that all it had been? A man who'd found her attractive? Somehow she didn't think so. His gaze had been too intense, almost probing. It hadn't been the gaze of masculine interest . . . it had been something much different.

By the time she was back home and fixing herself a light supper, she had almost forgotten the anxiety the man had caused her.

She took her salad onto the deck, letting the dogs out for their evening run. Frank had told her that morning that he expected it to be a late night at the hospital, so she knew she would have to entertain herself for the bulk of the evening.

As she ate her salad, a warm breeze drifted off the water, bringing with it the tangy salty scent she knew she would always remember when she looked back on this time in her life. That, and the tranquil rhythm of the waves breaking on the beach, would be the less painful ones to recall. The painful ones would be of Frank: his warm, sexy morning smile, the widening of his pupils just before he kissed her, the compassion in his voice as he spoke of his work and the patients that needed him.

She knew what she was doing...consciously preparing herself for the eventuality that she would have to leave here.

Stirring from her reverie, she quickly finished her salad and called to the dogs. She took a leisurely shower, then curled up on the sofa with one of Frank's mystery books. The dogs joined her at the foot of the sofa, one at her feet, and one just behind her in the crook of her knees. She knew they had her pegged as a soft touch, that she would allow them to join her on the sofa. But the moment Frank appeared at the door, they would be on the floor, looking innocent of all sofa-climbing crimes.

It took her only a few moments to become completely engrossed in the drama unfolding in the pages of the book. She didn't know how long she'd been reading when the dogs' ears pricked up and they both growled low in their throats.

"What's the matter, boys?" She set the book down on the coffee table as both dogs jumped off the sofa and ran toward the front door, their low growls continuing. Jane followed them to the door and peered out the small square window. Her breath caught in her throat as she saw a man getting out of a car parked in the driveway—the same man, the same blue car that he'd noticed earlier in front of the library.

With trembling hands, she quickly checked to make sure the door was locked, then she backed into the hallway and ducked into the darkened interior of her bedroom. She stood for a moment in the center of the room, her heart pounding frantically in her ears. What was he doing here? What did he want?

She could tell the minute the man stepped up on the front porch, for Mutt and Jeff went wild, barking their displeasure at the intruder's presence.

As a knock resounded on the door, Jane crept to her window, knowing from there she would have an unobstructed view of him. He was dressed in a rumpled suit and his hair was dark and neatly trimmed. As she watched, he knocked a second time, the knock assertive. He pulled a notebook and pen from his pocket and jotted something down, then turned away from the door and headed back to the car.

Long after he'd pulled off and disappeared, Jane remained huddled in the darkness of her room. He hadn't been a weirdo attracted by her smile, and he hadn't been a traveling shoe salesman. He'd worn the unmistakable air of a cop, or a private investigator.

Jane had no idea how she knew this, but the knowledge filled her with frantic, overwhelming fear.

Her insides clutched and her palms grew damp. He was a policeman and he was here to take her back to her life. He was here to force her to face her crimes. Tears coursed down her cheeks and she buried her head in her hands. She no longer had to worry about reaching deep inside herself and claiming her past. Her past was reaching out to reclaim her.

Chapter 12

Frank sat on a picnic bench in the center of the city park, watching Jane as she helped a group of women setting out food on a long table.

He stretched out his legs before him, relaxed and enjoyed the momentary quiet. Most of the townspeople were still lined up along the sides of Main Street, watching the last of the celebration parade.

He smiled as he remembered Jane's reaction to the parade. Initially, when they had left the house early that morning, she'd been quiet, rather withdrawn, and he had wondered what was going on in her beautiful head.

They'd made love when he'd finally gotten home the night before, but he had sensed a sort of desperation in her caresses, an intensity that had filled him with an

answering sense of anxiety. The anxiety had remained
with him through the morning, when she had seemed
so distant. He knew she wasn't telling him everything
about what she had remembered, knew she was
working through what memories she'd gained.

He'd been relieved when her mood had changed.
During the parade, her eyes had taken on their beautiful sparkle, and whatever had kept her distant and
preoccupied she'd obviously pushed away. Now, as she
helped Etta and the other women who had volun-
teered to take care of the food table, her laughter rang
out often and it was apparent she was completely at
ease.

The green dress she wore showed off her soft curves
and the luxuriant richness of her dark hair. She was
like a colorful butterfly flitting from group to group
of women, offering her help and her friendly smile.

"You're a lucky man, Frank Longford."

Frank turned and grinned at Russ, who planted
himself on the bench next to him. "Lucky?"

Russ winked at him. "Surely you aren't going to tell
me the situation between you and Jane is still completely innocent . . . not with the way you look at her
and she looks at you."

Frank smiled, his gaze automatically seeking her
once again. She was laughing at something Etta had
just said. Her head was thrown back, revealing the
slender column of her neck and the upward tilt of her
breasts. Frank felt an immediate burst of renewed desire. "No . . . not innocent," he replied, consciously
tearing his gaze away from her. His smile slowly faded.

"You've fallen for her." Russ stared at him in sudden comprehension.

Frank fought the impulse to protest, to laugh and tell Russ not to be ridiculous, that he and Jane were just having a good time, nothing more. But the falseness of it stuck in his throat and in an instant of self-examination, he realized what Russ said was true. He was falling for Jane Smith.

"Ah, Frank, how could you be such a fool?" Russ said softly. He looked over to her. "Granted, she's beautiful, and she seems genuinely nice. With any other woman I'd be thrilled that you've decided to try it all again. But you know the odds are good that when her memories return, she'll go back to whatever life she had."

"I know, I know." Frank released a sigh of frustration. "I seem to have a knack for getting involved with the most inappropriate women." He looked back at Jane, his heart constricting in his chest. "I know a lot of my patients think I'm nothing short of a saint...but she makes me forget all my good intentions. She makes me think the thrill of the moment is worth the gamble of the future."

Russ stared at Frank in amazement and released one of his telling low whistles. "Oh, man, you've got it bad." He stood up and clapped Frank on the back. "Well, I guess all I can tell you is to remember I'm around when she leaves and you need somebody to talk to. And if necessary, I can recommend the name of a terrific heart surgeon who might be able to put yours back together again."

Frank cast him another faint smile. "Thanks, I'll keep that in mind," he said dryly.

"Well, I see the parade must have ended," Russ said, gesturing toward the park entrance where a crowd of people streamed in. "I'd better find my lovely wife before she enters me in one of those crazy contests." With a wave, he moved away.

Frank immediately returned his attention to Jane, Russ's words echoing in his head. You've got it bad, Russ had said. "Yes, indeed," Frank murmured to himself. He had it so bad he was willing to risk the greatest heartbreak he'd ever experienced just to spend one more minute, one more day with her.

It was crazy. He knew in his heart she would eventually leave, that he would have to let her go. There was no way a woman as vibrant, as loving as Jane hadn't had friends and family, people who loved and cared for her. Yet, even knowing that she would leave him, he didn't have the strength to resist her.

She was an intoxication to his spirit, a drug to his soul, and even knowing that his withdrawal would be intense and painful, he couldn't fight his addiction to her.

He stirred restlessly, not wanting to think of the time when she'd be gone. He simply wanted to enjoy every second he had with her. He wanted to desperately cling to the moments they had left, savor each one of them to its fullest.

He smiled as she approached, shoving his thoughts aside. "Somebody said there's going to be a band playing in a few minutes," she exclaimed.

He nodded. "Over at the bandstand on the other side of the park. They play every year."

"Well, let's go." She pulled on his arm, tugging him up off the bench. He laughed, finding her enthusiasm contagious. Whatever had darkened her eyes and caused her soberness that morning was gone now, leaving her eyes luminous pools of dancing excitement.

As they walked toward the bandstand, Jane breathed deeply of the pungent air. It was filled with the mingling scents of fresh-cut grass, smoking meat and hot sunshine. It was a perfect day.

She had awakened that morning with a heavy sense of foreboding, feeling as if her time with Frank swiftly approached an end.

Throughout the morning parade, she'd scanned the crowds, looking for the man who'd come to their door the night before. She hadn't seen him anywhere and was finally beginning to relax. She wanted to forget all about him, forget all about her past. All she wanted to do was enjoy the day with Frank.

As they approached the bandstand, the band members were tuning their instruments, filling the air with discordant sound as they prepared to entertain the crowd that gathered on the benches and in the grass before them.

Frank and Jane joined the group on the lush grass, Jane not caring if she stained the skirt of the sundress she wore. She leaned against Frank, enjoying the softness of the thick grass beneath her, the strength of his shoulder beneath her head. Nearby, a group of children played, chasing one another around in circles, squealing and giggling in youthful abandon. Jane watched them, their laughter, their very enjoyment of life haunting her.

She closed her eyes as her head filled with the baby cries that tormented her in the dark hours of the night. Not now, she mentally begged, consciously shoving the haunting images, the eerie cries, back inside her brain.

As the band began to play a rousing song, she stood up and tugged at Frank's hand. "Come on, dance with me," she exclaimed, needing to lose herself in frivolity and activity.

"But...but nobody else is dancing," Frank sputtered in surprise.

"Then we'll get them started," she returned as she pulled him to his feet. It took only moments of Frank whirling her around to drive the horrors out of Jane's head. True to what she'd said, other couples joined them and soon there were a dozen or so twirling and stomping to the bluegrass rhythm of the music.

As the band played a slow, lilting melody, Jane moved into his arms and smiled up at him. "You're a mighty fine dancer, Dr. Longford."

"You aren't so bad yourself," he returned, tightening his arms around her.

Jane captured the sensations of the day in her heart, knowing this memory of Frank, of Garett Beach and of happiness would remain forever inside her.

The rest of the day flew by in a haze of laughter and fun. They ate smoked-beef sandwiches and cold watermelon slices, cheered on the participants in the races and giggled like errant teenagers as they stole kisses behind the bushes at the entrance of the park.

As evening approached and the sky began to darken, most of the townspeople gathered on a large, grassy hillside for the fireworks display to take place as soon as darkness was complete.

"There's somebody down there I should go say hello to," Frank said, gesturing toward a group of people halfway down the hill from where they sat. He leaned over and kissed her lightly on the cheek. "Don't move from this spot and I'll be right back."

She smiled and nodded, stretching her legs out in front of her, watching as he made his way through the crowd. He looked so tall and strong, so handsome in his pale gray slacks and crewneck shirt. She closed her eyes, a smile playing on her lips as she thought of the events of the day.

She had fallen in love with this town and its people, and they, in turn, had embraced her as one of their own. She knew part of the respect she'd received from the people was a direct result of her relationship with Frank. But part of it she had earned on her own, through her volunteer work at the hospital.

It was a heady feeling, to feel loved and respected by an entire community. It was even more exhilarating to feel desired by one single man. More important, he was a man who evoked both a wild desire and a quiet sense of companionship in her.

She opened her eyes and looked at Frank, surprised as she realized that she loved him. Yes, she loved him with every fiber of her being, with all the depth of her soul.

She'd admired him, depended on him when she'd first realized her amnesia and was lost, but somewhere along the line, her feelings for him had blossomed into full-blown, deep, abiding love. The realization struck her with a dizzying high, followed by a plummeting dive as she wondered what the future held for them both.

She pulled her gaze away from him and scanned the crowd around her. She grinned and waved at Cindy, who was with a group of teens at the foot of the slope.

She turned to look at the people on her left, smiling at the familiar faces, waving to people who called out to her in greeting. The smile on her face froze as she saw the man approaching her... a determined thrust to his shoulders, a grim expression on his face.

It was the same man who had been outside the library, the same one who had come to their door the night before. He pushed his way through the crowd, his gaze never wavering from hers.

Panic, raw and harsh, reverberated through her, causing her blood to pound loudly in her temples. She jumped to her feet, her thoughts scattered, frantic, not thinking of anything but escape... escape. He was coming to get her, and she was afraid of what he wanted, what it all meant. She stumbled backward, then turned and ran, vaguely conscious of outcries and curses as she stepped on, and tripped over people in her need to flee.

She paused momentarily at the top of the hill, pure terror obscuring her vision, muddying her thoughts. For a moment, she didn't know where she was, where she should run. Spying the park entrance, she headed in that direction.

She'd only run a few yards when she cried out as a hand clamped down on her arm, stopping her in her tracks. She turned and stared into the eyes of the man from the blue car. In them, she saw a recognition, a familiarity that terrified her. "No," she whispered, trying to jerk her arm away from his tight grasp. "No, please," she pleaded, afraid of who he was, what his role was in what she had done, what horrors he'd make her face.

"Jill?" A flicker of hesitation swam in the blue depths of his eyes. "It *is* Jill?"

"No...no, it's Jane. Please...please just leave me alone." She ripped her arm from his grip and whirled away. She didn't stop running until she reached the safety of Frank's car.

She tore the door open and climbed into the passenger seat, swiftly locking the doors, as if she could effectively lock out the passage of time, lock in all that she had to lose.

She wasn't even aware she was crying until she swept a hand over her cheek and discovered tears. She knew what they were...tears of mourning, tears of grief. The past was about to make a resounding impact on her life. She could only hide out from the man for so long. She could only run so far. But sooner or later, she had to face the crimes of her past.

She jumped as a fist thudded against the window. She looked up into Frank's worried, frantic face. She unlocked her door, gasping as he pulled her up and out of the car, directly against the broadness of his chest. "Jane, what happened?" His eyes scanned her face frantically. "Are you all right?" he asked, his voice a tortured whisper against her hair. She nodded, tears once again burning as they streaked down her cheeks. "Who was that man? What did he do, what did he say to you that made you run?" The questions burst out of him in a frantic staccato.

"Please, let's just leave. Take me home, please. Just take me home."

He nodded, helping her back into the car. Then he went around to the driver's side and slid in behind the wheel.

"Are you sure you're all right?" he asked once they were headed home.

"Yes, I'm fine now," she said wearily. She stared out the window, realizing she couldn't keep pretending that her past didn't matter. She couldn't pretend anymore that she could just blithely head into the future without knowing what she'd been, what she'd done, what horrors were contained in the dark recesses of her mind.

The death cries that haunted her, the nightmare visions that tormented her dreams and intruded into her thoughts had to be faced...and she would have to face the consequences of whatever she had done. She could run from the man who was after her, she could even run from Garett Beach, from Frank. But she knew she could never run far enough to escape her own conscience.

As much as she loved Frank, she realized that their love was no good as long as she feared and hated what she might have been. She touched the scar on the side of her neck, self-repulsion shooting through her. The scar was a physical reminder of her shame, the horror of her past. But it was nothing compared to the scars inside, and she knew the only way to heal them was to face her fears, face the blackness.

Frank pulled into the driveway and shut off the engine. Instead of getting out of the car, though, he turned and faced her, his features heavy with worry...and a faint touch of fear. "Jane, who was that man? Why did you run away like that? For God's sake please tell me what's going on."

She reached over and touched his face, loving the lines of worry, the concern and tenderness she saw shining from his eyes. She ached with the knowledge that she was about to tell him things about herself that would transform that caring into something ugly. "Come on, let's talk inside."

However, once they were inside the house, Jane realized she couldn't tell him about the fragments of horrible memory, not inside the house where she had fallen in love with him. Not in the rooms where they had laughed together and lived together and made love together.

She led him out on the deck, where the night wind embraced her and the soothing wooshing of the waves to the shore would be the only witness to her words.

"What's going on?" He caught her by the shoulders and deep within the darkness of his eyes, she saw a shadow of fear. "Who was that man?" he repeated urgently, his fingers tightening on her.

"I don't know who he is, but he's been following me." She stepped out of his grip and moved to the other side of the deck. "He was outside the library yesterday when I went in and he was still there when I came out. I was pretty sure he was watching me. Then, last night he came here. I didn't answer the door," she added hurriedly. "He knocked a few times, then finally went away." Her voice trembled as she continued. "Tonight, I saw him coming toward me and I panicked. He grabbed my arm and...and he called me Jill." She paused. "Jill," she repeated the name, somehow knowing deep in her heart that it belonged to her.

"Jill?" Frank said the name, his eyes searching hers.

"I think it's my name," she said in answer to his unspoken question. "It just...feels...right."

"But who was he? How does he know you?" Frank's anguish was in his voice, in the depth of his eyes as he stared at her. "Who was he, Ja—Jill?" The name fell stiffly from his lips.

"I think he's a policeman...or a detective."

"A policeman?" he echoed incredulously. "But why would a policeman be looking for you?"

Jane closed her eyes, a shiver sweeping through her as she drew a deep breath. She opened her eyes and gazed out into the distance, wishing she could fly away, disappear into the darkness of the night, do anything but destroy the concern she saw in his eyes.

At that moment, the sky burst into fiery color, signaling the start of the fireworks display in town. Independence Day. A bitter laugh of despair burst from her lips, a laugh that ended in a hopeless sob.

"Jane." Once again his hands fell on her shoulders, and gently he turned her to face him. His gaze searched her face intently. "Why would a policeman be looking for you?"

"Because I think I killed somebody." Tears oozed down her cheeks as she looked at him. "I think I'm a murderer."

Chapter 13

Her words hung in the air, and for a long moment Frank wondered if the wind had somehow distorted what he'd heard. But he could tell by the horror on her face, the tears that shimmered in her eyes that he'd heard correctly.

For a moment, his heart stopped, convulsed, then resumed a much more rapid beat. "What are you talking about?"

Once again she stared out into the distance, as if unable to meet his gaze. "I . . . I've been having nightmares . . . visions that I know are from my past." She shuddered and Frank fought his need to encircle her in his arms, chase away whatever visions she'd seen. She turned and faced him, her eyes luminous with tears. "There's a fire, and a baby crying and a man

urning to death. I don't know who they are or what
hey mean to me, but each time the visions end, I'm
eft with an overwhelming sense of guilt and the
nowledge that somehow I'm responsible for their
deaths. Each time I see these images, my hands are
overed with blood and smell like kerosene.'' She an-
rily swiped at her cheeks with the backs of her hands,
hen wrapped her arms around herself as if bitterly
hilled despite the warmth of the night.

She released a tremulous sigh. "I thought I could
ust continue to be Jane Smith. I wanted to be Jane
mith. I wanted to believe that whatever had hap-
ened was over and done, but you were right. I can't
o forward without going back and facing the events
left behind, whatever I might have done."

Frank frowned, unable to comprehend what she was
aying, what her memories might mean. He looked at
er, saw the vulnerable trembling of her mouth, the
yes that held shadows of pain. He knew this woman,
nd she was not a murderer. There was absolutely no
ay. He'd held her in his arms, made love to her, felt
er heart beating against his own. He knew Jane
mith and it was impossible that she was capable of
urder.

But he didn't know the woman named Jill. He
idn't know how she had been raised, what forces
ight have shaped her life, what circumstances might
ave forced themselves on her. But a cold-blooded
iller? Never. He simply couldn't believe it. And yet,
e couldn't deny the compelling evidence pointing to
e fact that she was guilty of something. As she re-

minded him of the fact that she had been using an assumed name at the rental cottages, told him that her hair was dyed, he felt a cold shiver of apprehension sweep through him.

For the next few minutes, he asked her questions, listening intently as she described the mental images, the horrible nightmares she'd been suffering. His heart ached for her, and hurt with a pain all its own. He didn't know what the memories meant, but they sounded frightening and ominous and caused an answering despair to ring inside him.

"What do you want to do?" he asked after she'd finished telling him everything.

She sighed, looking small and defeated. Then she inhaled deeply, raised her chin, and the inner strength he'd always known she contained inside appeared, shining in her eyes and straightening her shoulders. "I want to turn myself in to the police."

"But what good will that do?" he protested. It had been difficult to think of her in the shelter in Wilmington. It was impossible to imagine her in a jail cell.

"If I tell the police what I'm remembering, then surely they can figure out what happened, match my memories with the crime."

"Jane, it's not going to be that easy. We don't even know what city you're from, what state."

"That man who's been following me, he knows. I'll just turn myself in to him."

"We aren't even sure who he is," Frank objected. "I'm not going to let you just turn yourself in to anyone, some stranger we know nothing about." He frowned thoughtfully, feeling as if he'd been plunged into a bad dream, a nightmare from which he couldn't awaken. "Has Harry tried any sort of hypnosis with you?" he asked suddenly.

She looked at him in surprise. "No. He mentioned something about it last week, but I dismissed the idea. It frightened me. Remembering frightens me."

"But wouldn't it be better to remember before you decide to go to the police? Wouldn't you rather know what you're confessing to instead of just confessing to a bunch of confusing images that might add up to nothing?"

"I suppose," she agreed uneasily. She shivered once again. "Although they *don't* add up to nothing."

"I'll call Harry and see if we can set something up first thing in the morning. I still think you need to remember exactly what happened before you go to the police with stories of fires and murders."

As he went into the house to make the phone call, Jane leaned against the deck railing. She looked out to where the ocean sparkled, borrowing the colorful lights from the fireworks exploding overhead.

It was difficult to believe that only a short time ago she'd been sitting on a hillside, anticipating the joy of watching the fireworks with Frank. And instead, she had spent the celebration telling the man she loved that it was possible she'd killed two people.

As always, at thoughts of the baby and the burning man, her heart squeezed painfully in her chest and denial tore throughout her veins. How could I possibly have done something so terrible? How many times in the past couple of weeks had she asked herself that very same question? But still she had no answer, there could never be a rational reason for murder.

"Harry will meet us at his office at nine in the morning," Frank said as he rejoined her on the deck. He placed an arm firmly around her shoulders, pulling her into the strength and warmth of his body. "Maybe Harry can break through the amnesia with his hypnosis. Surely he can make some sense of this mess." His arm tightened around her. "You'll never make me believe that you're capable of those kinds of things," he said softly. "Never in a million years."

Jane closed her eyes against the burning press of tears. She welcomed his support, desperately needed him to believe in her innate goodness, but there was a part of her deep inside that didn't think she deserved his unswerving loyalty.

She turned around in his arms, looking into the dark eyes she'd come to love. She needed to physically feel the love she saw shining in their depths. She needed, one last time, to lose herself in the magic elixir of his arms. Before she faced the darkness of her past, she wanted to wallow in the splendor of the present. "Make love to me, Frank," she said softly. "Please make love to me."

Without a word, he walked with her into his bedroom. A shaft of moonlight danced in the window, along with the salty summer breeze that stirred the gauzy curtains. They undressed silently, not needing words between them to express the emotions that shone from their eyes, reflected on their features. The light sounds of the ocean rushed in the window, adding melody to Jane's whimpers of desire.

Where before their lovemaking had always held a frenzied passion, this time there was a quiet desperation, the knowledge that it might be the very last time they held each other, loved each other.

Their caresses were slow, memorizing strokes of heated flesh and kisses of bittersweet need. Jane lost herself in him, wanting his goodness and light to fill her up, wanting his love to stop the passage of time. She didn't want morning to come, knew that with dawn's light, she would be closer to having answers that could possibly take her away from him.

When their passion was finally spent, they remained entwined, their hearts thudding in unison in the darkness of the room. The night breeze swept across their bodies, causing a shiver to dance across Jane's body. Barely moving, Frank pulled the sheet up around them, as if cocooning them together in a fresh-scented cotton cave.

With her head resting in the crook of his neck and the warmth of his body surrounding her, Jane closed her eyes, mentally capturing his scent, his feel, his very presence in her heart. She had no idea what the dawn would bring, but somehow she knew that no matter what she found out about herself, things would never be the same between her and Frank again.

They spent the remainder of the night talking of inconsequential things: the weather, the picnic that day, their work at the hospital. Jane realized neither of them wanted to waste a single moment of the night by sleeping, yet neither said the things that were uppermost in their mind.

They didn't speak of fear or goodbyes. They didn't talk of murder or nightmares. They merely held on to each other, as if by willpower alone they could hold on to the night and keep the dawn away.

But as dawn swept its golden fingers into the bedroom, Jane felt an overwhelming sense of desperation grip her. She knew that today, whether through hypnosis or with the help of the police and the man who had been following her, she would learn her identity. But more important, she would face her nightmares, encounter the past in all its ugly reality. She eased herself out of Frank's arms, knowing he'd fallen asleep only a few minutes earlier. She'd let him sleep while she showered and made breakfast.

Before she left the bed, she paused for a moment, capturing his image to her like a miser clutching gold. She wanted to remember for an eternity his image above all others.

In sleep, his face held a boyish, innocent quality that touched the core of Jane's heart. His long lashes gave him an air of vulnerability that was contradicted by the strength of his cheekbones, the square cut of his chin.

He was such a good man. Was he good enough to want to remain involved with a woman who might have killed two people? No. She couldn't even ask that of him. He was a doctor, a healer of man.

She gently touched the side of his face, knowing that no matter what her life brought to her, Frank would always have a large chunk of her heart in his possession. Her memories of her time with him in Garett Beach would haunt her as vividly, as painfully as the memories that tortured her now.

With a sigh of anguish, she rolled off the bed and headed for the shower. She had to be ready to face what the day would bring. She had to be strong for herself, and she had a feeling she would have to be strong for Frank, as well.

"Relax, Jane. Just let yourself relax."

Dr. Wilton's voice was soothing, as was Frank's hand holding hers. She was aware of the scent of Frank's cologne, the soft ticking of the clock on Dr. Wilton's desk, the faint blowing of the air conditioner as it cooled the office.

She and Frank had been in there only long enough for her to tell Dr. Wilton about her visions...the memories she hadn't told him about before. The doctor had immediately sat her down and begun the hypnosis procedure.

"Breathe deeply, Jane. Let yourself go."

She did as Dr. Wilton asked, taking deep breaths as she felt herself falling into a floating, peaceful state. As if watching a newsreel, images began unfolding in her head.

She smiled, enjoying the scene that played in her mind.

"Where are you, Jane?" Dr. Wilton asked softly.

"A birthday party."

"Is it your birthday?"

"No...no, it's my best friend's party. All my friends are here...Alfie and Sally, Annie and Sandy...Teri and Marcia...we're having so much fun." She giggled. "Alfie pinned the tail on the donkey's nose."

"How old are you?"

"Ten. I'm ten years old, and it's Sally's party. She just turned eleven."

"And what's your name?"

"Jill. My name is Jill." The answer came with no hesitation.

"And what is your last name?"

Frank leaned forward, watching intently as she squirmed and frowned. He suddenly realized the incredible dichotomy. He desperately wanted her to remember who she was, and yet he was frightened for her, frightened for himself. He knew now the loss he'd felt when Gloria had left had been nothing compared to the devastation that would be left behind by Jane's abandonment. If she was going to remember something that would forever take her away from him, he didn't want her to remember at all.

"Jill, what is your last name?" Dr. Wilton repeated his question and her frown deepened.

"I...I don't know. I...I can't remember."

"That's okay," Dr. Wilton instantly soothed. "Let's go on, Jill. Go forward. You're twenty years old. And...older...older. You're now at the rental cottages in Garett Beach. What are you doing? What are you feeling?"

The happy expression that had decorated her face from her previous memory melted and transformed into a look of such hopelessness, such despair, that Frank wanted to halt the whole process.

He wanted to gather her into his arms and carry her away from here, away from the pain of whatever images were trapped within the depths of her mind.

She released her hold on his hand, clutched at the sides of her head with both hands. "Oh please... please make them stop." Her cries tore through Frank. He half rose from his chair. Harry sternly motioned him back down and he returned to his seat, watching helplessly as Jane cried out in anguish.

"What do you hear, Jill?"

She moaned, her eyes fluttering beneath their closed lids. Tears seeped out, sparkling like droplets of crystal against her sun-kissed complexion. A sob escaped her lips as her face twisted with whatever memory tormented her.

"Tell me, Jill. What exactly do you hear?"

"Death." The single word exploded out of her, hanging in the air for an infinite moment. "They're dying... burning up. Please... I don't want to hear it anymore. I... I just want them to stop." She paused for a moment, catching her breath. "I want to go away... disappear. I want to stop the noise in my head."

"Who are the people? What caused the fire?" Dr. Wilton shot the questions at her and Frank leaned forward, holding his breath as he waited for the answers to come.

"I... I can't. I don't... want." She opened her eyes and stared first at Harry, then at Frank. It was obvious she was out from beneath the suggestive power of the hypnosis. "I'm sorry. . . ." She clenched her hands together in her lap, looking at them helplessly.

"It's all right. You did very well," Dr. Wilton assured her. "Let's try it again."

For the next thirty minutes, the doctor put Jane under, only to have her surface each time his questions got too close to whatever trauma had caused her amnesia. Throughout the session, they had regained bits and pieces of Jane's former life, but the fragments were frustratingly superficial, offering no further clues to her identity, her past activities or self-alleged crimes.

"I think you've had enough," Dr. Wilton finally said, rising from his seat and patting her on the shoulder. "There's nothing to be gained by beating our heads against a concrete wall. Your internal protection is a formidable sentry."

Jane sighed hopelessly. "Isn't there something else we can do? Some other therapy or drug or something to force me to remember?"

Dr. Wilton shook his head. "I'm afraid, my dear, the only thing that will work is time itself."

"I'm afraid that's the one thing I don't have." Jane stood up, impatience and frustration battling with despair for dominance. She looked at Frank, knowing that the same kind of emotions raced through him.

It would be easy to fall into his arms, to beg him to take her away. She could forever bury the horror of her nightmares, keep them in the darkness where she would never completely understand them.

She knew she could use her love, use their passion to convince Frank to build a future with her despite her lack of memories, but it would be a future built on sand...with the waves of her conscience constantly washing away the very foundation.

She gazed at him, loving him enough not to subject him to a life with her...loving him enough to have the strength to face her past. "It's time to go to the police," she said, watching the play of emotions on his face.

He hesitated a moment, his gaze searching her features. "Are you sure?"

"No," she admitted. "I'm not sure about much of anything, but it seems that's the only avenue left." Her gaze sought his once again. "I can't continue like this...the not knowing has to be almost as bad as whatever I might have done. I've got to know, and I've got to face it."

"I must interject here and tell you that I don't think going to the police is necessarily a wise decision at this point," Harry said.

Jane smiled sadly. "Dr. Wilton, I'd say I have probably already made several unwise decisions that are going to forever affect my life." She didn't look at Frank, but knew that he would realize that she was talking about him, about the foolishness that had seemed unimportant compared to seeing through their passion...a passion that had transformed to love. "Fool's paradise...that's what I've been living here, but now it's time to face the morning light. I need to know the truth, and accept whatever consequences come with that truth.''

"At least let me go with you," Harry suggested. "As your doctor on record. I can address any questions the police might have concerning your amnesia."

Again tears filled Jane's eyes. "I'd appreciate it," she said.

"Thanks for your support," Frank said, echoing Jane's feelings, then placed an arm firmly around her shoulders.

As the three of them walked out of Harry's office and into the bright morning sunshine, Jane immediately stiffened in anxious expectation as she saw the man who had been following her for the past couple of days striding across the street toward them. Close on his heels was an older woman...a woman whose face Jane had seen for a brief instant in one of her flashes of memory.

Before the man could speak, the woman hurried to Jane, her face crumbling into tears as she engulfed Jane in a smothering embrace. "Oh, my girl, my darling girl," she whispered. "Thank God we've found you. Thank God you're all right."

As the scent of the woman's perfume wove its way into Jane's brain, with the familiar embrace of the woman's arms around her, Jane found her way back from the darkness. Her memory returned and as the horrors exploded in her head in vivid detail, she clung to her mother and sobbed.

Chapter 14

"Perhaps it would be best if we take this inside," Harry suggested, leading them all back into the privacy of his office.

"Maybe we should start by introducing ourselves to one another," Harry said once they were all seated in his waiting room.

Frank sat across from Jane, intently focused on her. She seemed to have pulled within herself, a remote preoccupied expression on her features. It scared him, the distance he felt from her, as if her past had already snatched her away and she was only a distant memory in his.

"I'm Victoria Sanderson, and this is my friend, Jacob Michaels. I hired him to find Jill." The woman clutched Jane's hand in hers, as if afraid that at any moment Jane might jump up and run away. "We've all been so worried about her...so very, very worried." She looked at Jane. "Why haven't you called? Why didn't you let me know that you were all right?"

"Jane—Jill collapsed on the beach outside my house several weeks ago. She's been suffering from amnesia," Frank explained, but as Jane looked up at him and he met her gaze, he knew she remembered everything.

Her knowledge glowed darkly in her eyes, changing them from the color of new spring to the dark mysterious hues of shadowed moss. Frank suddenly felt very much afraid.

"I'm Jill Sanderson and I was a flight attendant." Her voice was full of suppressed emotion. "I remember...I remember everything." Tears glistened on the tips of her lashes, like dewdrops on blades of grass. She drew in a deep breath and shuddered convulsively as she released it.

"Tell us, Ja—Jill. Tell us what you remember," Harry said softly.

She closed her eyes, leaning closer against her mother as if needing the support as she walked through the darkness in her mind. "We were on a flight from Florida to D.C." She frowned, rubbing a hand wearily across the expanse of her forehead. "I had a bad feeling from the moment of takeoff. It was just a bad day. The passengers seemed more cranky than usual, we discovered some of the lunches had spoiled and we had a colicky baby on board whose crying was making everyone crazy." Her eyes flew

pen and met Frank's, and in hers he saw intense re-
ef. "The baby... the baby from my dreams."

"Go on, Jill," Dr. Wilton urged her. "Tell us about
he plane."

"The baby's mother had her hands full with a two-
ear-old and a four-year-old. I tried to help her. I took
he baby, rocked him in my arms." Tears spilled down
er cheeks as she looked at all of them. "There was no
arning, no hint of any trouble at all. One minute I
as standing in the aisle rocking the baby in my arms,
nd the next moment I was on my back on the floor,
urrounded by darkness and chaos."

"Doctor... must she go through all this again?"
ictoria protested, obviously shaken by Jill's experi-
nce. "Wasn't the first time enough?"

Harry smiled gently at the older woman. "I think
oing through it all again is exactly what she needs."
e gave Jill a nod of encouragement. "Go on, tell us
hat you remember, what happened next?"

"I knew immediately what had happened," she
ontinued. "We had crashed. People were screaming
nd crying and I could smell smoke and fuel. I knew I
nd to get to one of the emergency doors and get it
pened." She shuddered convulsively. "I crawled
round, trying to get oriented, and finally did man-
ge to locate the emergency door. I opened it and
arted helping people get out."

"A real heroine she was, that was what everyone
aid," her mother interjected.

Jill continued as if she hadn't heard the older wom-
n's words. "All the time I was helping people out, I

could hear the baby screaming from someplace in the darkness inside the smoking plane. I knew I had to find her, had to get her out. She'd been in my arms when the plane had gone down. I was responsible for her." A sob caught in her throat and tears now ran freely down her face. "I could smell heat and smoke, knew there was a fire someplace and that it wouldn't be long before the whole plane exploded."

She paused a moment, swiping at her cheeks with the back of her hands. "I started back in to find her, but at that moment, a man came flying out toward me. He...he was engulfed in flames and...and it scared me and I hesitated, then it was too late. The fire was on me, burning me, and I fell out of the plane." She touched the scar on the side of her neck, her eyes tormented with the haunting cries of the baby she couldn't save. "Don't you see? It was my fault. It was all my fault that she died. I shouldn't have been holding her...and if I hadn't hesitated for that second or two, I might have been able to save her. It was my job to save everyone. It was my job."

"Or you might have died yourself." Frank left his chair and went down on one knee in front of her, his hand reaching to hold hers. "Jill, you were a flight attendant...not God. You did all that was humanly possible." He knew he was repeating her words back to her, the same words she'd used to comfort him on the night that he'd lost the three young patients. "Jill, you aren't guilty of anything, and you aren't responsible for anyone's death."

"But why do I feel so guilty?" she asked beseech-
gly. "That's been the one constant element in ev-
ything. I feel so guilty."

"Perhaps I can answer that," Dr. Wilton inter-
cted. "Jill, what you're suffering from is com-
only known as survivor syndrome. You feel
mehow guilty that you lived while others did not.
u've taken on a false sense of responsibility to as-
age the guilt of surviving. Unfortunately, it's a fairly
mmon phenomenon among people who endure a
rrific experience. Some survivors seek escape from
eir guilt by becoming alcoholics or drug users. You
ught yours by escaping your very identity."

"I don't understand any of this, sugarplum," her
other said, causing Jill to emit a shaky little laugh.
And I especially don't understand what you've done
your lovely hair."

"Oh, Mama, we have some catching up to do," she
id, then reached up and stroked the length of her
rk hair. "But I do remember dying my hair now. It
as right after the accident, right after I left the hos-
al." She frowned, remembering how difficult that
ne had been for her.

Nightmares had plagued her every hour as she re-
ed the crash over and over again in her mind. She'd
en suffering a deep depression she couldn't seem to
ake. "I just wanted to get away for a little while,
ve it all behind. I needed to be somebody else for a
ort period of time." She smiled reflectively. "It
ms silly now, but I thought if I could just take a

little vacation, change my hair color and use a differ
ent name, somehow eventually it would all be okay.'

She turned and looked at Jacob Michaels, who ha
sat silently in a chair in the corner throughout the en
tire meeting. "How on earth did you find me?"

He shrugged. "Your mother told me that wheneve
you had any free time, you liked to travel along th
Carolina coastline and stay in places near the beach
Thank God even in your trauma you didn't chang
your habit. It took me almost three months to finall
locate you here…and then I wasn't positive it was you
I had a picture your mother had given me, but it wa
an old one. You were a little heavier, and of cours
your hair was much shorter and lighter. I didn't wan
to raise your mother's hopes until I was positive it wa
you, and I wasn't positive until yesterday in the par
when I saw you real close. I called her last night an
told her you were here."

"I was traveling in Europe when the plane crashed,'
Victoria continued. "I didn't even hear about it unt
four days after the accident, and by the time I got bac
into the States, Jill had checked out of the hospital an
disappeared." She pulled Jill into her arms once agair
"I have been so very, very worried. You'd left most c
your things in your apartment. It was like you jus
disappeared off the face of the earth."

Jill smiled in apology at her mother. "I'm sorry
worried you. At the time I made the decision to leave
I'm afraid I wasn't thinking of anyone else but mysel
and my own pain. Besides, I've been very well take
care of by Frank. If it hadn't been for him, I don'

know what I would have done." She smiled at him as he released her hand and stood up.

"Well, I'm not the only one who was worried. David has been positively frantic, calling me everyday to find out if I'd heard anything."

"David!" Jill radiated a smile as she repeated his name. Her heart filled with the warmth his image evoked. "I have to call him, let him know I'm okay."

"Come on, dear, you're coming to my hotel room. You can call him from there." Victoria stood up, pulling Jill with her. "I don't intend to let you out of my sight again until I've assured myself that you're quite all right."

There was a sudden flurry of activity as the group once again moved outside into the brightness of the day. "Thank you, Dr. Wilton, for everything," Jill said, shaking his hand warmly.

"If you ever need anything, to talk or whatever, you know where to find me," Harry replied. "In fact, I'd recommend some follow-up counseling with somebody. You've been through quite a trauma, Jill. A few sessions with a good therapist wouldn't hurt." He squeezed her hand. "Just remember, you're not alone."

"I know that," she said humbly. No, she wasn't alone. She had a mother who'd been searching desperately for her, a town that had warmly embraced her and made her feel at home. But more than anything, she had a very special man who had supported her through the darkness.

Thanking Harry once again, she turned to speak to Frank. She looked around in surprise, suddenly realizing that at some point in the last few minutes he'd left. He was gone.

"Jill, sweetie, let's go," her mother called from the car.

Looking around one last time, Jill ran toward her mother and back into her life.

She was gone. Frank told himself that over and over again throughout the remainder of the day. He'd watched her drive away in her mother's car, and with her, she'd taken the best piece of his heart.

Already he felt empty, bereaved by the loss. He hadn't been able to face a formal goodbye. He hadn't been able to face the scene of her gratefully thanking him for all his help, reluctantly telling him she had her life back and would be leaving him now.

He was grateful that the horrors she'd lived through were over, finished, and no longer would her conscience tell her she'd done something terrible. He was glad she would be able to live with her memories now, and devastated that she wouldn't be living with him.

But he'd seen the way her face had lit up at the mention of that man's name. He'd seen the wild surge of joy, the elation that had lightened her eyes as his name had fallen from her lips. *David*. How was it possible to hate a man he'd never met? And how would it be possible for him to live the rest of his life without her?

He headed his car toward the hospital. Maybe he should get the name of that heart doctor from Russ, he thought dryly. Because he had a terrible pain in his chest, worse than a heart attack, worse than angina. He knew what it was—it was his heart breaking in two, and he also knew there was nothing he could do to stop the hurtful process.

The remainder of the day dragged by for Frank. He remained at the hospital until long after dark, reluctant to return to the silence of his empty house, reluctant to face sleeping in his big bed alone. He'd become so accustomed to having her around. She'd become a habit. He hadn't realized how lonely his life had been until she had filled it up, but now he felt the loneliness, the piercing ache of being completely alone.

However, the time finally came when he knew he could put it off no longer. It was time to go home, time to face that emptiness.

"You knew this time would come," he muttered out loud as he drove toward home. He remembered that first night, when he'd brought her into the hospital, when Etta had said that she was a fallen sparrow with broken wings. Well, Frank had helped mend her broken wings and it had been inevitable that she would fly away. And even though he'd known he was getting in too deep with her, the intensity of his pain shocked him, took his breath away.

He pulled into his driveway and sat for a long moment, his head resting on the leather of the steering wheel. Oh, how he wished he could develop a case of elective amnesia, wipe away from his mind the mem-

ory of every moment spent with her from the time he'
found her on the beach to the time she'd walked awa
from him today.

How blessedly peaceful it would be if everyone i
the world could simply forget the very existence of los
loves. How kind it would be if the remembrances o
passion, and desire, and love were no longer there t
mull over in lonely hours, to cause pain in the darkes
hours of the night.

With a wearied sigh, he got out of the car and wen
inside the house. He paused, closing his eyes in pai
as he smelled her sweet scent still lingering in the air
How long would it take before the house no longe
smelled of her presence, breathed of her essence?

He stepped into the living room and stopped dea
in his tracks. He stared at the vision before him, won
dering if perhaps she was just an illusion wrough
from his tremendous need.

She was on the sofa, sprawled in sleep, the dog
draped over her feet. What was she doing here? Ha
she simply come to pick up her things? Questions
fears—and hope—swirled inside him, for a momen
making it impossible for him to speak.

And for a moment he didn't *want* to speak. H
merely wanted to take the time to look at her, drink i
her beauty, capture her image forever in his mind. He
long dark hair draped itself across the pale sofa, teas
ing him with memories of its silky texture, its swee
scent. Her lips were parted, as if eagerly awaiting
lover's kiss. Her sundress had ridden up, exposin
those long, lovely legs that he loved to stroke.

Then he didn't want to look at her anymore. He was afraid to allow the hope that flared inside him any substance. She could simply be here to pick up her things and leave, he reminded himself sternly. Just because she was here didn't mean she was back to stay.

He leaned forward to shake her shoulder, to wake her up, but paused, deciding he didn't want to touch her. He didn't want his fingertips to register the softness of her skin. He didn't want his brain acknowledging the desire that even now pounded through his veins.

"Ja—Jill." He called her name softly, watching covetously as her eyelids fluttered, then opened to expose green depths.

"Hi. You're finally home." Her voice was the sleepy, dusky rasp that always created a warm burst of fire in the pit of his stomach.

"What are you doing here?" he asked.

She didn't answer immediately. She sat up, disturbing the dogs, who jumped down and immediately curled back up on the floor.

She shoved her dark swath of hair away from her face and smiled at him. "Why would I not be here? This is where I belong. This is my home."

Frank stared at her for a long moment, afraid that he hadn't heard the words she'd said, but rather had imagined the words he wanted to hear. "I don't understand," he said faintly.

She stood up and approached him, stopping when she was mere inches from him. Her floral fragrance surrounded him and the green of her eyes beckoned like the inviting sweet grass of spring. "Dr. Longford, you hired me as your housekeeper. Did you think I would just leave here without giving you any kind of notice?"

"Notice?" He looked at her blankly.

She nodded. "Most people give their employers a two week notice. I'm giving you the rest of my life."

"The rest of your life?" he echoed.

"If you want it." Her eyes shone with a love that wrapped itself around Frank's heart. Still, a remaining vestige of fear surfaced.

"But what about your life? Your work as a flight attendant? Surely you have reasons to go back, return to what you had before the accident."

She took his hand and guided him over to the sofa, where they both sat down. "I spent the afternoon talking with my mother, getting back into the skin of Jill Sanderson." She looked at him reflectively. "The rush of memories was so confusing at first . . . like an entire lifetime flashing instantaneously in front of my eyes. It was a bit overwhelming."

As she spoke, she held his hand and stroked his fingers with sensual caresses, seemingly unaware of the resulting fire she stirred in his blood. "I needed to sort out Jane's life and Jill's life, see what pieces I wanted to keep of both of them. But the more I thought about it, the more I realized there was very little of Jill's life I wanted back."

She stood up suddenly, pacing the floor in front of him. "At the time of the plane crash, I was already discontented with my life. I traveled most of the time, shared two apartments with four different women in two states to accommodate my work schedule. I was contemplating quitting my job and finding another one that would keep me in one place. I needed something more than what I had.'' She stopped pacing and looked at him. "I don't want Jill's life back. I want Jane's life...here, in Garett Beach, with you.''

"What about David?" Frank held his breath.

She frowned. "David? What does he have to do with this?"

"Well, it was obvious from what your mother said that you and this David were close before your amnesia.'' Frank felt the words sticking in his throat, but they were words he needed to say. He wanted her to be sure...very sure of her decision. He needed her to be definite about what she really wanted. "Jill, your time here at Garett Beach is so fresh in your mind, I don't want your gratitude and these most recent memories to get all tangled up in your mind so you deny the importance of your other life, the other people in your life.'' He gazed at her for a long moment. "If you decide to stay here...with me...I want you to be very sure and never look back with regrets.''

"Regrets?" She once again took his hand and tugged him up to stand next to her. "The only thing I would ever regret would be leaving here, leaving you.'' She wound her arms around his neck, her fingers gently caressing the hair at the nape of his neck. "And as far as David is concerned, of course we were very close. We still *are* very close. Frank, David is my brother.''

"Your brother?" An explosion of relief swept through Frank, as intense, as vivid as a celebratory fireworks display.

She nodded, pulling him closer against the heat of her body. "Frank, I want to be here with you, and Mutt and Jeff. I want to continue keeping your house and doing my volunteer work at the hospital. I want to be a part of Garett Beach, but more important, I want to be a part of your life."

"Oh, yes," he whispered into her hair, against the satiny softness of her cheek. "I love you," he exclaimed, saying out loud the words that had been beating in his heart for what felt like an eternity. "I love you, Jill Sanderson, and I want you in my life more than I've ever wanted anything."

"And I love you," she returned, laughing in abandon as his lips found hers and captured them in a kiss that promised forever.

"We just have one more tiny detail to work out," he said when the kiss finally ended.

"What's that?" she asked tremulously.

"I'm firing you as my housekeeper. I can hire anyone to clean my house." He smiled down at her, his dark eyes caressing her with a love that was tangible and rich. "I have another job for you...as my wife. Will you marry me, Jill?"

"Yes...oh, yes," she cried, her heart bursting wide open, overflowing with happiness. She'd needed a place to heal, a sheltered haven to stay until she found her way back from the blankness of her mind. Instead, she had found love, a love to last a lifetime.

She felt as if she'd been running for months, searching for the place where she belonged. And she'd finally found it here, in his loving arms.

Epilogue

Jill stood on the deck, watching the dogs run along the beach, their silhouettes darkened against the twilight that painted the horizon. She smiled in happy contentment as a lingering ray of sunlight caught and sparkled off her diamond ring.

Jill Longford. She'd been Mrs. Frank Longford for the past two months, and they had been the most wonderful months of her entire life. Their wedding had been attended by most of the townspeople and Jill's family. It had been a day blessed with friendship and love.

She turned at the sound of the door opening behind her. She smiled at her husband as he stepped out, holding two glasses of lemonade. He set the drinks down on the table, then motioned for her to join him on one of the chaise longues.

As she curled up in his arms, she sighed in wondrous satisfaction, enjoying his embrace and the salt-scented breeze that eased the heat of the night. Riding on the light wind was the sound of the wind chimes, ringing out the sweet melody of home.

"My last session with Dr. Wilton is next week," she finally said, breaking the peaceful silence.

"We'll have to do something wonderful to celebrate," he said, his fingers moving slowly, sensually, up and down her bare arm.

"We could always go to the movies and make out in the back row," she suggested, giggling as he delivered a resounding kiss on the side of her neck.

"We could always stay home and make out," he replied.

"True," she agreed, "and I have a feeling if we stay here and make out, you might just get lucky and score."

"Hmm, sounds like a celebration to me," he growled into her ear, making her laugh once again.

"Speaking of celebrations..." She eased herself out of his arms, smiling as he groaned in protest. She stood up, then motioned for him to join her at the railing.

When he stood next to her and she was enveloped by the spicy scent of his cologne, warmed by his intimate nearness, she pointed to where the stars were just beginning to wink their presence.

"Remember the night we sat out here and talked about the stars and unfulfilled wishes?"

He nodded and she turned to face him. "Well, I won't buy you a pony, and I can't give you a little brother or sister, but there is one wish I can make come true."

She smiled, watching as his eyes widened in stunned surprise. She nodded, taking his hands and placing them on her still-flat stomach. "A baby, Frank. It's true. I'm pregnant."

"A baby?" he echoed softly. His hands moved reverently across the flatness of her abdomen. "A baby." His eyes misted as he wrapped her in his arms. "Oh, Jill, I love you so," he said.

"And I you," she replied. She pulled herself away from him and gazed at him intently. "Promise me something, Frank."

"Anything," he replied.

"Promise me that if ever anything happens... anything horrible... I'll always remember you."

He pulled her into his arms, so close she could feel his heart beating in rhythm with her own, could fancy she heard the fragile sweet echo of the heartbeat of their child beating deep within her soul. "I intend to love you so long and so hard, it will be impossible for you to forget me." He kissed her deeply, then pointed to one particularly brilliant star. "That one's mine. The one you hung for me."

"No, it's ours," she corrected him, once again finding the comfort of his arms. "It's just a pale reflection of our love."

He smiled down at her. "Then it's going to be there a very long time . . . all of eternity." And looking into his eyes, she knew all of her past, reveled in her present and anticipated her future spent forever in his arms.

* * * * *

HE'S AN

AMERICAN HERO

He's a man's man, and every woman's dream.
Strong, sensitive and so irresistible—he's an
American Hero.

For April: KEEPER, by Patricia Gardner Evans:
From the moment Cleese Starrett encountered
Laurel Drew fishing in his river, he was hooked.
But reeling in this lovely lady might prove harder
than he thought.

For May: MICHAEL'S FATHER, by Dallas Schulze:
Kel Bryan needed a housekeeper—fast. And
Megan Roarke did more than fit the bill; she fit
snugly into his open arms. Then she told him
her news....

For June: SIMPLE GIFTS, by Kathleen Korbel: For
too long Rock O'Connor had fought the good
fight to no avail. Then Lee Kendall entered his
jaded world, her zest for life rekindling his former
passion—as well as a new one.

AMERICAN HEROES: Men who give all they've
got for their country, their work—the women they
love.

Only from

INTIMATE MOMENTS®

Silhouette®

INTIMATE MOMENTS®
™ Silhouette®

continues...

Once again Rachel Lee invites readers to explore the wild Western terrain of Conard County, Wyoming, to meet the men and women whose lives unfold on the land they hold dear—and whose loves touch our hearts with their searing intensity. Join this award-winning author as she reaches the POINT OF NO RETURN, IM #566, coming to you in May.

For years, Marge Tate had safeguarded her painful secret from her husband, Nate. Then the past caught up with her in the guise of a youthful stranger, signaling an end to her silence—and perhaps the end to her fairy-tale marriage.... Look for their story, only from Silhouette Intimate Moments.

**And now for something
completely different
from Silhouette....**

SPELLBOUND
R O M A N C E

**In May, look for
MIRANDA'S VIKING (IM #568)
by Maggie Shayne**

Yesterday, Rolf Magnusson had been frozen
solid, his body perfectly preserved in the
glacial cave where scientist Miranda O'Shea
had discovered him. Today, the Viking warrior
sat sipping coffee in her living room, all six feet
seven inches of him hot to the touch. His heart,
however, remained as ice-cold as the rest of him
had been for nine hundred years. But Miranda
knew a very unscientific way to thaw it out....

Don't miss MIRANDA'S VIKING by
Maggie Shayne, available this May,
only from

INTIMATE MOMENTS®
Silhouette®

It's our 1000th Silhouette Romance, and we're celebrating!

Join us for a special collection of love stories by authors you've loved for years, and new favorites you've just discovered.
Join the celebration...

April
REGAN'S PRIDE by **Diana Palmer**
MARRY ME AGAIN by **Suzanne Carey**

May
THE BEST IS YET TO BE by **Tracy Sinclair**
CAUTION: BABY AHEAD by **Marie Ferrarella**

June
THE BACHELOR PRINCE by **Debbie Macomber**
A ROGUE'S HEART by **Laurie Paige**

July
IMPROMPTU BRIDE by **Annette Broadrick**
THE FORGOTTEN HUSBAND by **Elizabeth August**

Silhouette Romance...vibrant, fun and emotionally rich! Take another look at us! And as part of the celebration, readers can receive a FREE gift!

You'll fall in love all over again with Silhouette Romance!

CEL1000

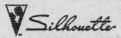